Praise for P

"If you prefer your Amish on the quaint and colorful side, *Broken English* is not the book for you. For in this, the second Ohio Amish mystery by P. L. Gaus, they are human beings, not picture postcards in a souvenir shop. . . . Here's hoping this series will be around for a long time."

— *Strand Magazine*

"*Broken English* is a well-developed, tightly plotted, keep-you-guessing mystery filled with the cultural richness of Holmes County."

— *Columbus Dispatch*

"Gaus weaves his extensive knowledge of Amish ways into this fascinating, suspenseful tale. There is a 'show-in-plain-sight' clue that will escape all but the most astute readers. The characters are differentiated and believable, from Sands, who feels 'no imposing moral dilemma' to Hawkins' Amish fiancée, who insists on Hawkins' innocence. This is a deeply felt, insightful book."

— *Ohioana Quarterly*

"A mystery man, rumored to have been trained by the U.S. military to kill, has settled in the Amish community and attempts to find peace there. When his only daughter is killed and the suspect is arrested, a wave of violence descends on the peaceful community and threatens to test the limits of friendship between the sheriff, Pastor Troyer, and Professor Branden. Another excellent addition to this series."

— *River Reader* (Lexington, MO)

broken
english

AMISH 🐎 COUNTRY MYSTERIES
by P. L. Gaus

Blood of the Prodigal

Broken English

Clouds without Rain

Cast a Blue Shadow

A Prayer for the Night

Separate from the World

Harmless as Doves

broken english

AMISH COUNTRY MYSTERIES

P. L. Gaus

Ohio University Press
Athens

Ohio University Press, Athens, Ohio 45701
© 2000 by P. L. Gaus
Printed in the United States of America
All rights reserved

New revised paperback edition 2020
Paperback ISBN 978-0-8214-1070-7
Library of Congress Control Number:2019957340

Ohio University Press books are printed on acid-free paper ⊚ ™

Library of Congress Cataloging-in-Publication Data
Gaus, Paul L.
    Broken English : an Ohio Amish mystery / P.L. Gaus.
        p. cm.
    ISBN 0-8214-1325-2 (acid-free paper) — ISBN 0-8214-1326-0
(pbk. : acid-free paper)
        1. Amish—Ohio—Fiction. 2. Amish Country (Ohio)—Fiction. I. Title.

PS3557.A9517 B76 2000
813'.54—dc21
                                                            99-086623

For my wife, Madonna

Romans 12:17–19

[17]Do not repay anyone evil for evil. Be careful to do what is right in the eyes of everybody. [18]If it is possible, as far as it depends on you, live at peace with everyone. [19]Do not take revenge, my friends, but leave room for God's wrath, for it is written: "It is mine to avenge; I will repay," says the Lord.

Contents

Preface   ix

Holmes County Route Map   x

A Journey to One of Holmes County's
    Highest Plateaus   xi

Broken English   1

Q & A with Author P. L. Gaus   207

Discussion Questions for Reading Groups   211

Preface

All of the characters and events in this novel are purely fictional, and any apparent resemblance to people living or dead is coincidental. The rifle range in this story is loosely patterned after the famous Kelbly benchrest rifle range on farmland in Wayne County, Ohio, beside the Dalton-Fox Lake road.

The author has strived to make descriptions of Amish life and thought as authentic as possible. The descriptions of places in Holmes County, Ohio, are true to life, although not all of the places are real. For those interested, the best Holmes County map can be obtained at the office of the County Engineer, across the street from the Holmes County Court House and the old red brick jail. Millersburg College is entirely fictional.

All scripture cited in this novel is taken from the Holy Bible, New International Version, Copyright 1973, 1978, 1984 by the International Bible Society, and used by permission of the Zondervan Publishing House.

Music verse courtesy of Ian Tyson, Slick Fork Music.

I am grateful for the assistance of Mr. Robert Eggles of the New Jersey Department of Corrections, George Kelbly, and Holmes County Sheriff Tim Zimmerly. Thanks also to Dean Troyer, Eli Troyer, and Madonna Gaus. Special thanks to Skip McKee, Bravo Battery, 3BN, 18 ARTY, Chu Lai.

I am especially grateful for the excellent and tireless work of my editors, David Sanders and Nancy Basmajian, and of Richard Gilbert, Sharon Arnold, and Judy Wilson, all at Ohio University Press.

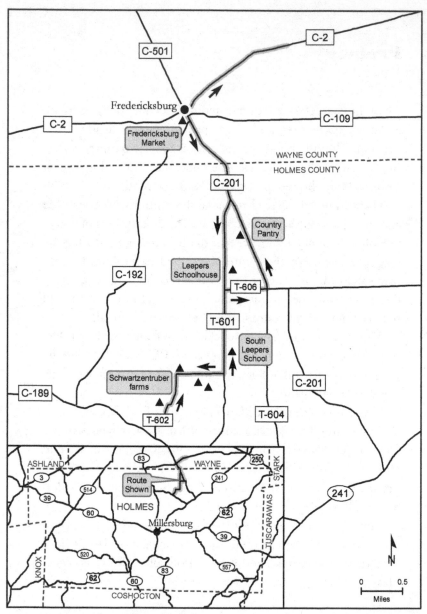

Map by Brian Edward Balsley, GISP

A Journey to One of Holmes County's Highest Plateaus

Fredericksburg, Ohio, lies close to the border between Holmes County and Wayne County. This quaint little village sits in a pocket at the intersection of Wayne County Road 501 and Township Road 2. At this intersection, there is a wonderful little general store called the Fredericksburg Market. If we proceed southeast from there on Wayne County Road 10 (South Mill Street), it will switch near the top of a steep hill to Holmes County Road 201, and after 1.2 miles, Salt Creek Township Road 601 turns off to the southwest. The journey along TR 601 is beautiful, and you'll want to travel slowly to be able to take in the long vistas and the many fine details on an Amish farm. Leepers School, a one-room red brick schoolhouse, is delightful, with its playground, softball diamond, outhouses, woodshed, and the old shack across the road, where the current teacher usually stables her buggy horse. The route south on 601 takes us past windmills, purple martin houses on tall poles, a red neighborhood Amish phone booth with solar panels, and several Amish businesses. For instance, we will pass a factory making Eco-Bricks for wood-burning stoves, a farm that sells handmade baskets, and a lumberyard and sawmill at another Amish farm.

As we continue south on TR 601, the more modern South Leepers School is on the east side of the road, and after we have traveled a total of 3.2 miles from the center of Fredericksburg, the high plateau comes up. Here is a good place to stop for the vistas. It is the location I chose in *Broken English* for the first meeting between Abigail Raber and Professor Branden. There are Schwartzentruber farms all around, with their typical tobacco-red barns, and the observant traveler can often spot sixteenth- and seventeenth-century-type iron farm implements that have been left out in the fields.

Take the turn west onto TR 602, and drive for a little bit on this route, passing more Schwartzentruber farms. When you find a safe place to turn around, head back to TR 601, and turn north to retrace the route toward Fredericksburg. Drive slowly this time, and take in the sights. There are sure to be things you missed on the first pass over this road. You can find another interesting Amish store, the Country Pantry, by turning east on TR 606 (which you will have passed earlier), taking this back out to County 201, and turning north. The Country Pantry will come up on the west side of the road. Then head back to Fredericksburg on 201 for the end of the trip. But if you are more adventurous, at the main intersection in the village, head east on TR 2, which is Harrison Road, going nowhere in particular, other than into more of the intriguing Amish countryside.

1

The middle of May

JESSE Sands, twenty-five years in the New Jersey State Prison for rape and felonious assault, had served a full term, without credit for either good or industrious behavior. From the ages of twenty-two to forty-seven, his home had been a cold prison fortress of brown stone and razor wire, built one hundred and fifty years ago in a resolute age when prisons had been intended to punish criminals. For twenty-five steadfast years, the Trenton prison had done its duty regarding Jesse Sands. Then, abruptly, once he had maxed out on his original sentence, he was turned loose without parole. The red iron doors swung open for him at 10:30 A.M., and by nightfall he had bought a gun on the streets and exacted his first harsh measure of revenge.

In the three weeks following his release, Sands had headed west, across Pennsylvania and West Virginia, to the Ohio River at Steubenville, where he thumbed a ride at night over the river and continued along Route 22 as far as the eastern Ohio burg of Cadiz. There he caught a ride with a truck driver, and, after sleeping in the cab as they traveled at night, Sands pistol-whipped the trucker at 4:00 A.M. in the bathroom of a deserted rest stop along US 250, dragged him into the woods beside the road, shot him in the back of the head, and stole the rig.

Sands drove west on 250 until dawn and abandoned the truck in a lot behind a Burger King at New Philadelphia. After walking several miles in the morning, he flagged down an unwary farmer north of Dover, and they traveled together peacefully until Sands got out at Wilmot. He lunched there at an Amish restaurant and then started walking through the countryside along Route 62, heading southwest toward Winesburg, Berlin, and Millersburg. As he stalked the Amish colonies of Holmes County, he caught rides with two unsuspecting tourists and, toward sunset, with a kindly Amish youngster coming home late from sparking his sweetheart in a buggy. By the time Sands reached the sleepy hills of Millersburg, it was nightfall on a rainy Saturday in May, and a report had gone out to the sheriffs in several eastern Ohio counties about a murdered truck driver at a rest stop and his abandoned eighteen-wheeler, found in New Philadelphia with most of the gears ground out.

That night, in a steady downpour, near a west-end neighborhood bar in Millersburg, Jesse Sands stood rock-still in an alley, eyeing the houses along one of the narrow streets that marked the western limit of town, overlooking the Killbuck Creek and its broad and marshy floodplain beyond.

From his position pressed flat against the weathered boards of an old garage in the graveled alley, Sands worked his eyes methodically, first in one direction and then in the other. He waited there motionless, watching the comings and goings at a neighborhood bar at the end of the street. His collar was turned up tightly against the back of his neck, and the night rain dripped off the front brim of his rumpled, black rain hat. He was dressed for the night in black jeans, dark brown workboots, a lightweight black windbreaker over a dark blue pullover shirt and black sweater.

There was the constant pelting of the rain against the galvanized tin roof, the clatter of running water in the downspouts, and the occasional splash of tires on the street as a car eased along in front of him. In time, the splatter of rain on his hat put a thin line of cold water under his collar. It trickled down his back between his shoulder blades. He took his hat off, slapped it against the rough boards of the garage, and pulled it back over his damp hair, then stood rigidly against the boards, ignoring the rain as he watched the bar at the end of the street.

The front of the bar was lit by a floodlight at the top of a wooden pole. The building was an old house, sided with wood shingles stained dark green. The shingles covered all of the windows on the front of the structure. Facing the street, there was otherwise only a steel door with a small diamond-shaped window at about head level. Where there once might have been a lawn, there was now a gravel parking lot that surrounded the bar on three sides. Two cars and a pickup were parked in front, taking a neon glow in the rain from a Budweiser sign that hung out near the street.

After deciding to enter, he moved quickly across the gravel lot underneath the floodlight, stepped up onto the old porch, turned his collar down, pushed through the heavy door past two cigarette machines, and stood just inside the door, waiting for his eyes to adjust.

As he scanned the smoky room from the doorway, Sands slowly removed his hat, ran his fingers through his curly hair, and forced a slight smile. He managed a steady and confident expression, standing with his feet close together, holding his dripping black hat loosely in his fingers at his side.

Along the right wall in a single first-floor room was a series of four booths with puffy black Naugahyde upholstery. Sands counted: Three men at the first booth. A man and a woman in western dress at the second booth. A young couple at the third booth, getting ready to leave. The fourth booth was empty.

The bar itself ran along the opposite wall of the room. No one was seated on the five padded stools there. The bartender stood quietly eyeing Sands, while polishing a glass with a white towel.

The bartender was short and muscular, and he wore a white apron strapped tightly around his waist. The sleeves on his plain white T-shirt were rolled up to his shoulders, showing tattoos on each arm, anchors with serpents. Good, Sands thought. Serpent-arms won't be the talkative type.

Sands took a seat at the far end of the bar, laid his wet hat on the barstool to his left, and looked directly ahead at the whiskey bottles on the shelves, his back straight. The bartender lingered more than a polite moment while he lit a cigarette, pulled on it unhurriedly, and laid it deliberately in an ashtray next to the cash register. Then he moved slowly toward Sands, dragging a towel to polish the surface of the dark wood as he approached. Five feet from where Sands had taken his seat, the bartender stopped and waited, looking directly at Sands without speaking. Sands ordered without glancing at the bartender, "Two drafts now and two more later."

Two draft beers, in heavy frosted mugs, were silently delivered, and the bartender resumed his place at the other end of the bar. Sands drank one of the drafts down straight away and tuned his ears to the conversations in the booths behind him. Normal, he thought. Steady, quiet voices. They had taken note of him, but they now seemed willing to ignore him. He could drink alone. He'd be able to think. Think about the few needs and rare pleasures that still mattered to him.

For Sands, there were no imposing moral dilemmas. No work appointments, no family obligations, no friends and no troubles. Neither were there any long-term plans to be made. There was only the money, running low now despite his string of robberies. He needed more, soon, and that was all he knew. That was all he cared about. Perhaps this would be the town, he mused, where he'd finally stage a daylight bank job.

Sands took a cigarette out of his windbreaker's inside breast pocket, snapped a silver Zippo open, and lit up. He watched the room in the mirror behind the bar, exhaled heavy smoke from a Camel straight, absently spit a few grains of loose tobacco off the tip of his tongue, and returned to his beer. As he drank down the second one slowly, Sands began to relax, and his mind wandered from present needs to former pleasures. Someday they'd find that trucker, but he didn't care. The girl in the pickup truck had been easy. They might find her truck, but they'd never find her. A satisfied smile crossed his face. He had a boyish look sitting there, but his jaw was set hard, and his eyes were narrowed to slits as he drank alone and thought.

How many houses had he broken into? A dozen, maybe? Child's play, picking out the easy ones. Then there was the rush, the surge of power as he prowled through a darkened house, sometimes finding the owners at home, sometimes waiting in the dark until they returned.

For several quiet minutes at the bar, Sands held his memories closely, and then a burst of laughter from one of the booths behind him snapped him back into the room, and his mind returned to the question of banks.

Banks. Even in the daylight, they were surely better than houses. He sipped on his beer, lit another cigarette, and gazed thoughtfully ahead.

For sure, robbing houses was a nuisance. And finding a fence for what he stole was a bother. Risky. Always troublesome in strange towns. Stores and banks would suit him better. He glanced briefly along the bar to the cash register and wondered if bars would be good for him, too.

In time, Sands lit another smoke and finished his second beer. He pushed the two empties forward on the bar and turned his head to see if the short bartender had been watching. Two more frosted mugs were delivered, promptly, along with the tab. The bartender's gaze remained fixed on Sands slightly longer than could be considered warm and friendly. He slid the tab forward, flipped his towel over one shoulder, and returned to his end of the bar near the cash register.

Not so subtle, Mr. Bartender, Sands thought. Four beers and out, is that it? No problem. He'd find a place to stay, and then tomorrow he'd study the town at his pleasure.

He finished the two beers quickly, threw the money, with no tip, on top of the green and white paper tab, and spoke from his end of the bar.

"Where's the john?"

The bartender moved slowly along the edge of the bar toward him, swept off the money, and answered without turning away, "In the back."

When he was finished, Sands slipped out through the back delivery door into an alley. He took several deep breaths of the night spring air. The rain had stopped, and he stuffed his rain hat into an outside waist pocket of his windbreaker. The dampness held the chill in his legs. Maybe he'd just forgotten. Cold spring weather. A permanent chill that creeps into your bones. He drew another deep breath of the damp air and set off in the dark to walk the stiffness out of his legs.

He moved rapidly away from the bar, into a narrow alley that led through a neighborhood of old houses. His legs and arms soon responded to the pace, and the cold air invigorated him in a way that had never been possible in the confines of prison. This was the part of freedom that surprised him the most, walking wherever he chose, always quickly, as far as he liked, sometimes spending hours moving through the alleys and back streets of an unfamiliar town. By the time he had reached Ohio, he had realized that he could cross the country in this manner. When he made it to the mountains out west, he intended to climb up somewhere high, alone, and spend a day looking down on a city, or out across some prairie, enjoying the long vistas he had forfeited in prison. He'd be able to see forever. To enjoy being alone, high up and in command. Choosing for himself the moment to drop down onto a town.

Tonight, as he moved along the alleys of Millersburg, the

cluttered backyards and closely packed wooden garages presented themselves to him silently, and his instincts began to quicken.

A broken-down hard-shell camper had been parked at the back of one yard, and weeds had grown up under it. The next yard was surrounded by a fence of slat boards and rusty wire, and there was a swing set with an old bicycle leaning against it. The sections of a dismantled TV antenna tower lay along the fence, bent wires of the antenna stacked on top. Farther along, an overturned charcoal grill lay next to a picnic table with a plastic ice chest propped upside-down on its hinges. At the next house, the garage had slipped off its foundation and was leaning heavily out of plumb. Three of the four windowpanes were broken out, and as he passed, Sands saw that the door had been taken off its hinges and propped against the side of the garage, where weeds had overtaken its bottom edge. At one dark section in the alley, Sands stumbled on a rake handle and fell next to a disorderly pile of garbage cans, garden hoses, and the rusted hulk of an old wheelbarrow. He cursed himself for the noise and then paused there on his hands and knees, listening intently.

The alley ahead was lit at an intersection by a streetlight. He knelt just out of range of the light and studied the backyards lit dimly by its beam.

There were plastic lawn chairs stacked next to two galvanized garbage cans. There was a plastic child's swimming pool filled with rainwater. Against the side of the nearest garage was a stack of salvaged bricks, most still edged with mortar. At the back of the opposite garage was a cast-off water heater. Sands glanced back along the stretch of alley he had just covered, half expecting to see someone he recognized, knowing that he never would. Then he rose and walked quickly under the light, across the intersection, and into the alley beyond, where a block of five darkened houses awaited him.

He approached the first house in near total darkness, covering the yard quickly, crouched over in a run, feet splashing across the water-soaked grass, head narrowly ducking under a wire clothesline that ran from the house to a pole in the yard. He tried the back door, but it was locked. No problem, he thought, just move on to the next one.

The next house was also easily approached. He slipped across a darkened, blacktop driveway that separated the two lots. He was there in seconds, and at the back of a white, wood-frame house, Sands found a porch with a screen door that wasn't latched. That was all the opportunity he ever needed. The sort of thing he'd always dreamed about in prison.

He was inside in seconds, and, moving slowly in the dark, he felt his way across a small back porch with a noisy wooden floor, and then through a kitchen, a swinging door into a dining room, and a living room. His prison ears served him well as he stood motionless, listening in the dark until his eyes adjusted to the faint street light coming through a front living room window.

The house smelled peculiar to him, maybe old. He'd find two retired fools upstairs, he thought, and take everything they had of value. He made himself think calmly and planned his first night in Millersburg. He could work here for maybe an hour as the owners watched, forcing them to surrender cash, jewelry, whatever pleased him. Maybe he'd kill them.

He felt intensely alive as he found the steps to the bedrooms upstairs. He had his revolver out in his right hand. He reached out with his left hand and felt the smooth, worn wood of the handrailing. His feet moved slowly and methodically on the plain wooden steps. The revolver's heavy weight calmed him, as he eased up the steps.

Abruptly, there was a noise downstairs. It stopped him on the steps. A screen door squeaked open and slammed shut against its wooden frame. The floorboards of the back porch gave out their careless noises. His ears worked acutely.

A light came on in the kitchen. He could see its glow outside on the driveway through a window on the stairway landing. He turned his head slightly, his mouth open to enhance his hearing. His pulse rang in his ears, and he decided to risk another step on the stairs, descending closer to the noise. But as he turned and started down in the dark, his boot missed the step, and he tumbled sideways down the stairs, struck his head on the closet door at the bottom, and blacked out for a brief moment.

When he came around, Sands fumbled for his gun on the hardwood floor, found it, and struggled to stand. A sharp pain in his ribs dropped him to his knees, and he groaned heavily. As he pushed his way to his feet, with the revolver in his right hand and his left arm wrapped over his broken rib, Sands heard the sounds from the switchhook of a phone, followed by three short taps. A woman's voice in the kitchen spoke urgently, "911?"

In the living room, Sands tried the front door. It was locked. He fumbled to work the lock, but it was the dead bolt kind that requires a key. The woman on the phone seemed closer to him now, as she spoke briskly in the kitchen. His instinct was to flee, but his head throbbed and his ribs ached from the fall, and it angered him. And he realized coldly that there would be several minutes before he heard the sirens.

He turned from the door and peered into the shadowed dining room. He thought of the kitchen. He could still hear the woman back there, blocking his way. The light went out.

He moved slowly toward her. He imagined her up close. He could hear her voice on the phone. No police, yet. He had time. He'd take time. He held his left arm across his aching ribs, and, crouched over in pain, with his revolver still clutched in his right hand, he advanced toward the voice on the phone, unaware that he had been groaning all along.

He was in the living room. Now the dining room. Moving toward the kitchen. The phone receiver clattered onto the floor.

He was at the swinging door into the kitchen, with a sense of menacing power surging through him.

Then, in a shattering instant in the dark, as he pushed through the swinging door, a wooden chair broke across his face, cutting and stunning him. He had not been prepared for the blow. It simply exploded in his face, and he knew she would fight. Again, before he could react, there came a second vicious blow from the chair, this time striking him across his chest. The pain surprised him. Rage enhanced the effect within him.

He staggered backward under her blows, into the dining room. She pursued him in the dark, swinging the chair furiously. He retreated into the living room, and still she pushed her attacks with the chair, screaming at him. For a brief moment he slipped free of her attack. He couldn't see her, but he could hear her approaching again and raised his gun.

He fired a shot into the dining room, and the muzzle flash gave him his first view of a young woman in a yellow raincoat, hood down across her back, short hair wet, caught in the muzzle's burst of blue and orange light, with the chair raised over her head, surprise on her face, stunned by the explosion. He had missed.

He could hear her backing up, now, against the dining room table. She tossed the chair into a corner and fled back to the phone. It was a mistake.

He advanced on her. He caught her in the dark and jerked her back into the dining room. She struggled in his grip, clawing, hammering, and pushing off to free herself. He could smell the new rain in her hair when he cracked the heavy revolver across her face, knocking her into the corner of the dining room. Broken glass and china showered over her as she sprawled against a hutch, and Sands figured for a brief moment that that would be the end of it.

But as he stepped free of her, wiping blood off the side of his face with the back of the hand that still held his revolver, she came at him again. And he shot her. Twice. In the chest.

The muzzle flares from his .44 magnum lit her up in two rapid flashes of light. The second one caught her stumbling backward, lifted nearly from her feet, shock and dismay on her dying face. As her body crashed into the shattered glass in the corner near the broken hutch, Jesse Sands's eyes were imprinted with the glimpse of her seeming to hover in the air, his mind stunned by the horrific explosions from the magnum revolver in the confinement of the small, dark room. And she was dead before Jesse Sands had ripped his way through the back screen door.

But before he had cleared the steps on the back porch, while one foot still reached out for the lawn below him, with the image of crimson blood on vivid yellow lodged in his mind, and with the faint sounds of approaching sirens, Sands's forehead exploded into an infinite brightness, where colors flashed brilliant behind his eyes and shattered to white, like crystal on a black marble floor.

2

Tuesday Night
Several days later

JESSE Sands lay back smoking on his cot in a second-floor cell
of Millersburg's old red brick jail on Courthouse Square. He
was dressed in an orange prisoner's jump suit, the buttons undone to his waist, his ribs strapped with tape. He rubbed at the
light red hairs of his chest, grew tired of the cigarette, and flipped
it at the toilet, not bothering to check where it landed. In a scattered pile around the toilet lay a dozen half-finished smokes
from that night, with lines of ashes and brown tar stains on the
concrete floor where they had burned out.

As he lay dozing, the black metal door at the end of the line
of cells opened with a clank, and three men came up to his cell.
With a practiced scorn, Deputy Ricky Niell said, "You have
visitors, Sands," and stepped back down the hall to stand at the
metal door.

Sands eased up on an elbow, cranked his neck around toward the front bars of his cell, and saw a tall, blond man in his
fifties, dressed strictly Amish—dark blue denim trousers, white
cotton blouse with string ties, black cloth vest, and summer
straw hat. Next to him stood a shorter man, with long white hair
and full white beard, dressed in blue jeans and a work shirt.

"I'm Pastor Troyer," the shorter man said.

Sands flopped back onto his cot and said, "Don't need no
pastoring, Preach."

"I'm not here as your pastor, Mr. Sands. I've brought a friend. This is Mr. David Hawkins. Father of the girl you murdered."

Sands sat up on the edge of his cot and studied the two faces on the other side of the bars. The Amishman appeared nervous, but also stern. The pastor stood casually, peaceful.

Troyer stepped closer to the bars and said, "My friend has something to say to you, Mr. Sands." He eased the Amishman somewhat closer to the bars and waved a go-ahead.

The Amish Hawkins said, "You killed my daughter," and halted, uncertain. Perhaps unresolved.

Sands scowled, lit another smoke, and said, "So?"

"So," Hawkins said, "I forgive you." His hands trembled and tears coursed his cheeks and spilled into his beard.

Sands stood up, faced the bars purposefully, and blew smoke at Hawkins. Hawkins closed his eyes, struggled for will, and said again, "I forgive you, Mr. Sands."

With satisfaction, Troyer laid his strong hand firmly on Hawkins's shoulder and gave a soft, encouraging squeeze. He turned and left Sands and Hawkins facing each other through the bars, and he walked back to Ricky Niell at the end of the cells.

"Thanks, Ricky," Troyer said. "This will put David a long ways down the road to getting over his daughter's death."

Niell nodded, said, "No problem."

At the bars, Sands said something in a low, scornful tone to Hawkins, and Hawkins moved closer. Sands came forward and appeared to whisper through the bars. Hawkins stiffened, listening intently, and then cried out. Sands laughed aloud. In an instant, Hawkins had both arms through the bars, fingers locked on Jesse Sands's throat.

Sands wrestled to free himself, kicking at the bars and pulling down on Hawkins's wrists, but the Amishman's grip held firm. Niell ran up to Hawkins and pulled hard on his shoulders, and then his arms, ineffectively. Sands started to sag, and his throat gurgled painfully as he fought for breath.

Niell pulled his weapon and planted the muzzle on Hawkins's temple. "Let him go," Niell barked, and Hawkins slowly turned his head to glower at Niell.

"Let him go!" Niell shouted, and cocked the hammer on his pistol.

Abruptly, Hawkins pushed Sands back from the bars, withdrew his arms, and swung his right arm up and over Niell's pistol. In an impossibly short fraction of a second, he acquired the pistol, pinned Niell's back against the bars, and thrust the gun into Niell's face.

Cal came to Hawkins's side and said, "Let it go, David."

Hawkins said, "You don't know what you're asking, Cal."

"I do," Cal said. "Let it go!"

"Not now," Hawkins said vehemently.

He pressed his thumb tightly against the side of Niell's neck and caught him under the arm to lower him to the floor. He eased the hammer down on Niell's pistol and handed the loaded weapon to Troyer. Finally he said, "You don't know what you've asked me to do," and disappeared through the metal door at the end of the hall.

3

Saturday, May 31
5:30 P.M.

SO *the Bromfield kid got his story. Well then, that tears it wide open. Reporters never learn.*

His plane arrived at 4:05 this afternoon, and that'll put him here any time now. Of course he'll come to the newspaper offices. Just wait him out. Deal with him when he gets here.

OK. Run the weapons check. The .45. The .38. The .22. The silencer. Easy now. There's his car. Walk over slowly. Stay casual. Time it to meet him as he gets out of the car. Smile. Not too fast. Good. He's not running. Excellent.

"Mr. Bromfield, I'd like a word with you."

"I'm sure you would, but I don't think so," Bromfield answered, walking around the front of the car.

"Look. I know that you're interested in the Sands case. How about I buy you dinner and tell you what I know? That sound all right to you?"

Eric Bromfield stopped and turned. "I've got the whole story now, so you're pretty much all washed up."

How foolhardy Bromfield is, standing arrogantly in the alley, when he should be running for his life. Check all around. Is there anyone else here? Walk slowly toward him and reach for the .22.

Slowly. Don't spook him.

"How about it, Bromfield? You can have it as an exclusive."

"What makes you think I need to talk to you? I've been doing some checking, and I've got all the facts I need."

This is too easy. Make as if you're leaving. Shrug as if you couldn't care less. Start walking away and make it look as if you expect nothing more natural than for him to follow you into a deserted alley, like any good reporter who has a new lead.

Turn, now, to face him.

"Come on, Bromfield. Just half an hour."

Good. He's at the passenger's door. No need to talk now. Just five paces back to the car. He'll pull out the keys and fumble with them for one second. Everybody does that. Walk up to the car door as he bends to open it. There it is. Almost done.

Now step up. Stop shaking. Don't let him see your face. He'll read your eyes. A tap on his blind shoulder. OK, there, that did it. Reach behind the sport coat. There's the Ruger .22. Steady. Don't rush it. Just as he turns. One second more. There it is. Smoothly draw it. Up to the temple. Pop. Pop.

Now hold his arm. Keep him upright for just a second more. Turn him and ease him into the passenger's seat. That's it. Now close the door. Keys are on the ground. OK. Around to the other side. Scan quickly. Did anyone see? Is anyone looking?

Good. Into the car. Hold him up. Let his head rest against the back of the seat. Slowly now, drive away. Smile, in case anyone sees. Talk to Bromfield as if he still can hear.

4

Sunday, June 8
3:00 P.M.

DEPUTY Sheriff Ricky Niell found himself on the hills of
Millersburg College shortly after commencement exercises had
finished. He pulled his cruiser into the shade of the tall college
oaks, near the street where Professor Michael Branden lived
with his wife Caroline in a two-story brick colonial on a cul-de-
sac just off the college grounds. He switched off the engine and
reported his position to the weekend dispatcher down at the
old jail.

As he waited for the professor to come along the sidewalks
in the east end of town, Niell's thoughts turned to firearms. In
particular, one very modern and deadly firearm. Niell was interested in it because Sheriff Robertson was interested in it. A
.22 automatic, likely fitted with a silencer.

According to Coroner Taggert, it had been held close to the
left temple of Eric Bromfield, something like a week ago, the
first two bullets snapping his head right. Then later, another
shot from the same .22 automatic, this time into the base of
young Bromfield's skull, piercing the brain stem. They had found
the body yesterday, and the sheriff's indignation had been
nearly boundless.

Sheriff Robertson faced two homicides, now. There had been
the Hawkins girl in her own home, back on May 15, and now
there was the young reporter, Eric Bromfield. Consequently,

Bruce Robertson's changeable personality had swung into a manic phase, and the deputies at the jail were paying a heavy price for his displeasure.

Niell spent twenty minutes near the college, watching the graduates and their families pace their routes into the dorms, out to their cars, and back. While they wrestled boxes into cars, the professor appeared on the lawn under the oaks, his gold-tasseled, blue velvet tam still balanced on his head, his gown and hood draped casually over one arm.

He was dressed in a faded gray suit, white shirt, and red tie. Patches of his wavy brown hair poked out from under his tam. He had a thoughtful look in his eyes as he strode along under the tall oaks and the few surviving wide and majestic elms that lined the streets near the college. A graduate ran up to him on the street, shook his hand, talked for a moment, and gave him a hug before returning to the dorm.

The professor stood watching the students for a while. When he turned to walk again, his light blue eyes watched the old familiar brick sidewalks as he eased along toward home. His collar was undone, and his tie was loosened. With the summer come at last, he'd likely dress in nothing more than blue jeans and T-shirts for the next three months. He'd get into a pair of hiking boots, break in a new summer hat, take up a rod or two, and angle his way through the weeks, resting his mind from the classes.

His full brown beard, trimmed close, showed a touch more gray at the temples than Ricky remembered from the year before. His thin nose wrinkled with a thought, and he stopped and turned briefly to look back toward the history building.

When Branden made the turn onto his dead-end street, Niell pulled his cruiser around the corner, popped a short yelp on his siren, gave his top lights a brief whirl, and rolled slowly along, matching his speed to the gentle strides of the professor. Niell tapped fingers to his forehead in salute from his seat behind the wheel. Branden laughed and waved Niell ahead toward his house. Niell drove to the end of the street, swung around to about eleven o'clock in the circle, and parked in front of the Brandens' old house. He switched off the engine, got out, straightened his uniform, and waited on the tree lawn beside the cruiser for Branden to arrive.

Branden turned onto the short brick walkway to his front porch, and offered Niell his hand, saying, "Ricky. It's been too long."

Niell grasped his hand and said, "How are you, Professor?"

The professor spotted an envelope in the black, cast-iron box mounted on the bricks beside the front door. He lifted out the envelope and let the lid drop with a metallic squeak and clank. He motioned for Niell to follow, pushed through the white screened door, and led the way along the cool front hall, opening the envelope as he walked.

They came out through the kitchen and an adjoining family room, onto a spacious back porch, where Caroline Branden sat working over a manuscript at a glass patio table. She rose from her work and held the professor tightly for more than the usual moment's embrace. She was nearly half a head taller than the professor, trim, and had long auburn hair, tied back in loose, flowing curls. She was dressed in blue jeans and an old, over-sized, green and white Millersburg College sweatshirt. She carried a quality of soft and gentle peace, a gracefulness that could never be masked by baggy clothes.

Niell came onto the porch with a display of genuine shyness, crossed to her, and offered his hand. She turned from her husband and gave Niell a hug, saying, "You're looking good, Ricky." Niell blushed and stepped back a bit, unnerved by her smile and her warmth.

His crisp black and gray deputy sheriff's uniform lay close against his sturdy frame, long creases pressed meticulously down the front of each breast pocket and down his uniform slacks in unbroken straight lines to his cuffs. He wore his full black leather duty belt, with gun, flashlight, pepper spray, handcuffs, and a double magazine pouch. On his chest, he sported gold badges, gold insignias, gold collar stays, and gold pens. His black hair was cut short in a flattop, and his narrow black mustache was trimmed straight above his thin lips.

Caroline turned back to Branden and asked, "How was commencement?"

"The usual," Branden said. "A couple of seniors didn't graduate, and there was a thank-you note from one of my advisees." He dropped the note onto the table, and laid his tam beside it.

Caroline turned to Ricky. "Ricky Niell, you still look better in a uniform than any man has a right to do."

Niell felt an intense embarrassment and hoped silently that she'd turn back to her husband. But she held his eyes for a playfully long moment and asked, "You and Ellie still an item?"

He nodded, shy but more confident now.

The professor remarked, mischievously, "It's been a while, Deputy. Has our sheriff gotten himself squared up with the FBI over last summer?"

Niell quipped, "You'd expect Robertson to admit he's got a problem with the FBI?"

"No more than I'd expect him to care if he did," Branden said, and motioned Niell into a white wicker chair near the windows of the long porch.

Caroline offered drinks and left to get them. Branden stood at the tall screens on the back porch and gazed absently toward the eastern hills of Amish country. They lived two short blocks off campus, near the easternmost cliffs of Millersburg. Their boxy colonial stood out near the sidewalk in a neighborhood that had always been considered a part of the campus, where a succession of faculty had lived close to their students for a hundred years.

The Brandens' front yard consisted of two small patches of

lawn, with a brick walk that ran a few paces to a small front porch. By contrast, their enormous backyard opened out onto a double-wide lot at the back of the street's dead-end circle. The lawn sloped away for nearly fifty yards before the sheer drop-off into the valley, and the view from the Brandens' full-length, screened back porch was a spectacular panorama of Amish fields, houses, and barns. The professor had long ago improved that view by taking down nine trees on the lot, several days after Caroline's second miscarriage. Several days after learning that she would never be able to have children.

Abruptly, Branden turned from the screens and asked, "Ricky, I don't suppose it'd be too much to hope that our sheriff has gotten himself into some sort of entertaining little scrape with an irate band of citizens?"

"No more than usual," Ricky said, and laughed.

Caroline came back onto the porch with a tray of soft drinks and iced tea.

"No committees. No ACLU lawyers? No student protesters?" Branden asked, as Niell accepted a can of Pepsi. Branden took a tall glass of tea.

Caroline sat in a wicker chair with a matching glass of tea and asked, "Is it Bruce again?"

Niell shrugged an apologetic "yes" to Caroline's question, and then answered the professor, "Apparently not."

"Has he fired another secretary? Has Ellie Troyer quit?" Branden pushed, enjoying himself, partly joking and also serious, expecting something new and entertaining to have surfaced in the sheriff's broad and churning wake.

"We've still got Ellie out front," Niell said.

Branden teased, "And you two still an item."

Caroline protested for Niell, "Already asked and answered."

Branden waved her off and held Niell's eyes with a boyish grin.

"Something like that," Niell said and settled self-consciously into the wicker. "What are the chances, Professor, that you'll run into Cal Troyer later today?"

Branden sat up a bit. "We've always gone fishing together after I'm done with commencement. I haven't spoken to Cal in several weeks, but I expect I'll see him at our usual pond sometime this afternoon. Probably about three or four. Maybe later. Why?"

"You haven't talked with Troyer in a while?" Niell asked.

"Not for several weeks, maybe more," Branden said and waited. He glanced over to Caroline and looked back to Niell.

Niell asked, "Do you know about Janet Hawkins, the young woman who was killed in her home by an intruder last month?"

Branden looked at Caroline again, curious, and said to Niell, "Like anyone else, we read about it in the papers. Convict released from a New Jersey prison. Broke in late at night and shot her. He was captured in her backyard as he fled."

"Captured by a retired security guard," Niell said.

"The way I remember the write-up," Caroline said, "it was a close thing. The man heard the call on the police-band radio in his car, realized he was pretty much in the area, and got there before the cops arrived."

"Right," Ricky said. "Knocked him out cold with a baseball bat."

"Is there more?" Branden asked. "Seems straightforward enough to me. Even if he hadn't been there, the police were probably only minutes away. Probably would have caught the guy anyway."

"It's not the security guard," Niell said.

"Then what?" Branden asked.

With a rueful gaze, Niell said, "Sheriff Robertson's got a wild hair that I should find David Hawkins, Janet Hawkins's father."

"Why?" Branden asked.

"The sheriff thinks Hawkins knows something about a second

murder we discovered yesterday. A young reporter. Robertson considers Hawkins a suspect."

"And why does he consider it your job in particular to find Hawkins?"

"Because I should have grabbed him up at the jail one night and didn't."

Branden's eyebrows tented.

"Troyer was there the night Hawkins got away," Niell said. "I'm hoping you can help me find Troyer. Hoping Troyer can produce Hawkins."

"Cal Troyer ought to be the easiest man in Millersburg to track down," Branden said.

"There's a note tacked to the door of his church saying he's gone to harvest this week," Niell said in the tone of a question.

Branden remembered Cal's practice of helping with the wheat or barley harvests, sometimes with haying, and replied, "He works on some Amish farms this time of year. Says he likes to stay in touch with the land. To help friends he has in the Amish areas."

Niell nodded. "I need to find him, Professor," he said. "Need to find him because I've got to round up Hawkins and bring him in."

"Again, Ricky, why?" Branden asked. "What connection could the murdered woman's father have with this other killing?"

"Robertson thinks Cal's friend David Hawkins is involved in some kind of revenge scheme that includes the murder of that reporter," Niell explained. "And he thinks Cal knows where Hawkins is."

Branden rolled his eyes. With extreme confidence he said, "Cal Troyer is not capable of scheming revenge for anything. For anyone. For any reason. Robertson ought to know that better than anyone."

"You don't know the whole story," Niell said quietly.

Branden eased back against the soft academic robe that he had hung loosely over the chair. He laid his forearms along the broad white wicker armrests, and said, with his eyes and his posture, "I'm listening."

Niell began. "A couple of days after the girl was murdered, late one night when I was on duty at the jail, Pastor Troyer came in with the murdered girl's father and used his clergy pass to the jail to talk his way past me, to let them see Jesse Sands."

"That's the ex-con who killed the girl?"

"Right. We pulled him up off the lawn beside the girl's back porch. Anyways, Cal Troyer showed up at night, at the jail, with her father, David Hawkins, an Amish fellow. At least he was dressed Amish. They said they had come to see Sands. They just wanted to stand outside his cell on the second-floor blocks and say that Hawkins had forgiven Sands for the murder of his daughter. Very emotional, profound. You could tell it was the genuine thing."

"Second floor, with the individual cells?"

"Right."

"And you let them in?"

"Troyer's got a clergy pass. Hawkins was a judgment call, but not too risky knowing the Amish. I took Troyer's word that there'd be no trouble." Niell smiled weakly and added, "Now Sands's lawyer wants me brought up on charges of violating his client's civil rights."

Branden nodded sympathetically. "So what happened?"

"Well, I watched them for a while from the other end of the cell block. Troyer and Hawkins stood well back from the bars and just seemed to talk quietly to Sands. Sands lay on his cot, grinning like he enjoyed it, like it was some kind of perverse spectacle. After a couple of minutes, Troyer left Hawkins and Sands alone at the cell and came over to me. He said something about how he appreciated the gesture.

"Then Sands stood up to the bars and whispered something

to Hawkins. Him dressed criminal and Hawkins dressed Amish, and nothing but the bars between them. We didn't hear what he said, but the next thing I knew, Sands started laughing. Scornfully. And then that Amish Hawkins was at the bars, both arms through, grabbing Sands by the throat.

"I tried to pull Hawkins off, but nothing doing. Sands went limp. I put a gun to Hawkins's head and cocked the hammer. Hawkins turned his head, looked stone dead at me along the barrel, and released Sands. Sands dropped to the floor of his cell, gasping, and the next thing I knew I was looking back at the muzzle of my own gun. It had happened so fast that I couldn't be certain, even now, how he did it. But there he was, pressing the muzzle against my forehead. He said something to Cal like, 'You don't know what you've asked me to do,' and disappeared."

"What do you mean, he 'disappeared'?"

"Professor, he has vanished. He did something to my neck that dropped me to the floor, and disappeared. When I came to, Cal Troyer was kneeling beside me, holding my gun."

"And where is Hawkins now?"

"Nobody knows," Niell said. "At least nobody who's talking. But I figure Troyer knows, and that's why I'm looking for him."

"Does Robertson know that Hawkins took possession of your duty arm?"

"No. Cal's never mentioned it," Niell said with obvious relief. "Neither have I, and I'm trusting you won't either."

The Brandens quickly nodded assurances. "Has David Hawkins done anything to harm Sands in jail since then?" Branden asked.

"No."

"So why are you so anxious to find Hawkins?"

"Like I said, there's been another murder. We found the body yesterday, off the road in a thicket beside Lower Sand Run. He was Eric Bromfield, a young reporter for the *Holmes Gazette*."

"What's the connection?"

"The reporter had evidently been working on the Janet Hawkins murder. His editor has most of Bromfield's early notes."

"Marty Holcombe?"

"Right, and Holcombe's got the first parts of a story that Bromfield had written. Holcombe reported Bromfield missing a week ago and said Bromfield never turned in the finish to that story. Holcombe hasn't run it because Bromfield evidently had cracked something wide open. Told Holcombe he had a show-stopper, but he never made it back to the newspaper offices."

"I know Marty Holcombe," Branden said. "How does any of this connect to David Hawkins and Jesse Sands?"

"We found the reporter in the passenger's seat of his own car. He had two rounds in his left temple and one in the back of the head. Twenty-two caliber bullets. The coroner says he's been dead about a week. That means he was killed just before he would have filed the finish to his story.

"We've been through his apartment and his desk at the *Gazette*. Mostly routine stuff. Notes on stories, things like that. But one big story was set to run in several parts in the weeks to come, starting with how David Hawkins's daughter was murdered by Jesse Sands. More to the point, it was going to be a big exposé about who David Hawkins really is."

Branden waited, leaning forward on the armrests of his chair.

Niell paused a moment and then continued. "The reason that Sheriff Robertson wants Hawkins is tied to what we've found out about Troyer and Hawkins. Robertson considers Hawkins a suspect in the murder of Eric Bromfield, because of what Bromfield had learned about Hawkins. And I'm counting on Cal Troyer's knowing where Hawkins can be found."

Branden thought a spell and then asked, "Cal Troyer took Hawkins to the jail to forgive Sands?"

"Right."

"Did he?"

"Did he what?"

"Forgive Sands."

"Don't know. Didn't hear any of their conversation."

"But you do know that eventually Sands stood up, moved close to the bars, whispered something and then laughed, and that before it was done, Hawkins had Sands by the throat and you staring down the barrel of a gun. Your own gun."

Niell shrugged morosely.

Branden continued. "Then the reporter, Eric Bromfield, got to nosing around in the matter, and Robertson thinks something Bromfield discovered gives Hawkins a motive to have murdered that reporter."

"Right."

"So what did Bromfield discover?" Branden asked. "What does Bruce Robertson consider the motive to be?"

"Bromfield learned that David Hawkins moved here nine years ago. Wife was divorced and long gone, and we think she's dead. Hawkins had his daughter living with him out on the west end of town. She had a degree from Ohio State in English. She came back home when he moved here, and worked as a secretary with a metals fabricating outfit up in Wooster. Hawkins was retired. Partly, he came to Millersburg to retire to a quiet life in a sleepy, country town. Also, Hawkins apparently moved here because of Cal Troyer. He came to Millersburg to attend Cal's church."

"How does this all connect up with Jesse Sands and a murdered reporter?"

"Robertson thinks Hawkins murdered Bromfield because Bromfield figured out what Hawkins had been doing before he moved to Millersburg. He thinks Hawkins wanted to hide his past."

Branden waited.

Niell continued. "Hawkins knew Troyer in Vietnam. They didn't serve together, but their paths evidently crossed."

Niell rose from the white wicker chair, moved to the tall

screened windows, poked his thumbs under the front of his duty belt, and looked out eastward for a spell. He ran a palm over his short, black hair, and then he turned from the screens and explained. "After I reported the incident with Hawkins in the jail that night, Robertson did some checking. He thinks Bromfield did the same thing, finding out about Hawkins.

"Robertson has learned that David Hawkins was part of a U.S. Army Special Forces team. Part of an elite unit. After Nam, that unit continued its operations in various parts of the world, as a counterterrorist team. We think he worked for the CIA, and Sheriff Robertson wants him brought in."

After Caroline had seen Niell to the door, Branden stood gazing out through the screens, eyes trained on the distance, for almost an hour. In the end, he was disinclined to believe that Cal Troyer would be involved in anything even remotely resembling a revenge scheme. Branden found himself incapable of holding murder and Cal Troyer together in a single coherent thought. His eyes wandered the distant hills, and he also found it profoundly unthinkable that Cal would harbor any criminal, much less a murderer.

Two murders in less than a month, and Niell hoping Cal could talk Hawkins into coming down to the jail. Could Cal do that? Not if Hawkins were guilty. And what was that about Hawkins being dressed Amish? It didn't fit. Nothing did.

He finished the tea as he stood on the back porch. He thought again about everything that Niell had said, and scowled at the tangled mess the deputy had brought him.

David Hawkins, Special Forces, now missing. Cal Troyer, country preacher, material witness. Sands, ex-con held for the murder of Janet Hawkins. Sheriff Robertson, suspecting Cal of being involved. Eric Bromfield, reporter, murdered. And the reason? Was it as simple as Robertson had figured? Murder a reporter for nothing more than an upcoming article?

David Hawkins was an Amishman. Niell had said that plainly

enough. But how had Hawkins made the change from U.S. Special Forces to Amish?

And Hawkins's English daughter? Shot in her home the middle of May, and now evidently the pivot point in an entirely different case, the murder last week of the reporter, Eric Bromfield.

Satisfied that he had the facts and names in place, Branden slumped into a wicker chair and marveled at the larger question. Did Cal Troyer really know that the "Dutchman" he had taken to the jail to forgive Jesse Sands was, in a prior life, a soldier in the U.S. Army Special Forces?

5

Sunday, June 8
3:30 P.M.

CALEB Troyer was on the water by midafternoon the day of Branden's commencement exercises, easing slowly around the pond with a fly rod and a popper. It was an unusually warm and windless Ohio spring day, and with a bright sun, there was not the slightest wave or ripple on the surface of the water.

Cal was dressed casually in blue jeans and a dark blue cotton pullover. His flowing white hair normally resembled the style of an Amish bishop's, though considerably longer, but today he had it pulled back in a short tail. His full white beard was prominent, set off distinctly against the tan of his rough and leathered face.

Since the day his grandfather had quit an Amish sect more than fifty years ago, none of the Troyer men from Caleb's line had worn the traditional Amish beard, trimmed and shaved smooth around the mouth. Instead, as if to emphasize the distinction in a county where only the locals would notice the difference, Cal Troyer's mustache was long, and trimmed to the curve of his lips. Still, his short arms and legs gave the impression of the small Dutch stature of his Amish heritage.

His arms and hands were massive and strong, since, in the hours between Sunday sermons and Wednesday evening services, Troyer earned his living as a carpenter. That is, he earned a living when he wasn't building things free for friends or family in need.

Under the bright sun that afternoon, Cal worked the fly rod high overhead in strong, confident strokes, elbows held close to his ribs. The pole lifted slowly up and back, and the line followed in an arching ballet. The leader and popper came off the still surface gently, softly, and then picked up speed at the end of the line, sailed back overhead, wrapped into a tight curve at the end of its run, and came on gracefully with the forward stroke of Troyer's arm. The thick orange fly line laid itself out straight, and the clear leader followed softly. At the end of the thin leader, the popper settled delicately onto the water and lay motionless.

Cal held it there, about a foot off the bank ahead of him, and then, after a suitable spell, he gave the line the slightest of taps, and the popper's rubber legs twitched. Almost immediately, there came a surge under the lure. The line disappeared, and Cal lifted the rod to twelve o'clock to set the hook.

The line shot down into the water, came up directly, and darted erratically left and right several times. The pole took the surges overhead, pumping under the strain on the line. When the bluegill eased off, Cal brought it in flat, along the top of the blue water. Landed, it lay straight in his palm and completely covered all of the outstretched fingers of his hand. The little lips were even with his fingertips, and the tail stretched back as far as the middle of his forearm. On its flank, it flashed the colors of a thousand iridescent hues, gills pumping the air, eyes wide in alarm. Cal removed the hook, put the bluegill on a stringer with a dozen others, and wound line back onto the reel.

When Mike Branden arrived, he took note of Cal's fly rod and wordlessly chose a lightweight, open-bail spinning rig for himself. This choice defined the terms of the afternoon's competition. It wasn't lost on Cal.

Branden tied on a small spinner bait with a feathered tail and a Colorado blade. After they had worked silently, side by side, for nearly an hour, the professor admitted defeat and switched to a fly rod, too.

"I expected you earlier," Cal said.

Branden tied on a black and yellow popper, nipped off the end line with his teeth, spat it out, and said, "We finished up with commencement pretty much on time, but I had company waiting when I started home."

"Anyone I know?" Cal asked and landed another.

Branden made a cast, set his hook on a sunfish, and said, "Ricky Niell."

"Oh?" Cal asked, sounding only slightly surprised.

"Do you know he's looking for you?"

"I imagine it's more like Bruce Robertson who's looking for me," Cal said.

"It sounded serious to me," Branden said. He tossed the small sunfish back into the pond and held his eyes on Cal.

"Not really," Cal said and strolled along the bank to a new spot behind a stand of cattails. Branden followed.

"You want to tell me about it?" Branden asked.

"Look, Mike," Cal said, "there's nothing there. Robertson's running around half-cocked, again, that's all. Just like when we were kids."

Branden sat down on the bank near Cal and asked, "Then do you want to tell me about David Hawkins?"

"He was a member of our church."

"Nothing more?"

Cal stopped fishing and turned back to Branden. "I'm sure you know that David Hawkins's daughter was murdered," Cal said. "The fellow who did it is a guest at the county brick house."

"Did you also know that Eric Bromfield, one of Marty Holcombe's young reporters, was found murdered yesterday?" Branden asked.

"No," Cal said, disquieted. "Is there a connection?" Cal stepped over to the professor and sat down on the high bank beside him. "What's this got to do with David Hawkins?"

Branden explained. "Bruce thinks that Bromfield was working up a series of articles about how Jesse Sands murdered Janet Hawkins."

"So?"

"So, in the process, Bromfield looked into your guy Hawkins and uncovered his past. Now Hawkins is missing, Bromfield is dead, and Robertson surmises that you know something about all of that. In particular, he thinks Hawkins killed Bromfield to stop his stories, and he considers you to be a key witness, because you know where Hawkins can be found."

Branden studied Cal's eyes. Cal shook his head, seeming disappointed. Then Cal said, "I do know where Hawkins is."

"Are you going to tell Bruce Robertson?"

"Nope."

"Why?"

Cal fell silent for a moment and said, "Because David Hawkins cannot have murdered anyone."

"Hawkins was a soldier, Cal."

"I know that well enough. That was in the past," Cal said forcefully.

"Ricky Niell says that Hawkins took Sands by the throat the night you two went over to the jail."

"That doesn't mean he's capable of murder."

Branden acknowledged that with a nod and said, "Do you know what set Hawkins off? What Sands might have said to him through the bars of that cell?"

"No."

"Then how can you be sure that Hawkins hasn't flipped?"

Cal shrugged a silent but confident answer.

"Could Sands have whispered something that would have blindsided Hawkins? Something about the murder of his daughter that we don't know?"

"David Hawkins will not have murdered anyone," Cal asserted softly. "I'd stake my life on that. David Hawkins is a changed man. Has been for nearly seven years."

"Then why not tell Bruce Robertson where Hawkins is?"

"I wouldn't tell anyone, least of all Bruce Robertson."

"Then how about me?"

"Not even you, Mike," Cal said. He sat back and closed his eyes against the sun and the stress. A silent moment passed with Cal on his back, eyes shut, thinking. Branden sat on the bank and fiddled with his line. The sun broke low under Branden's cap. Barn swallows and martins dropped out of the afternoon sky and made their strafing runs over the surface of the pond, snatching bugs. The slightest of warm breezes stirred, promising summer.

Eventually, Cal said, "OK, Mike, suppose I do the next best thing. I'll introduce you to his fiancée. If she wants you involved, she can take you to Hawkins herself."

"Today?"

"Tomorrow. I'll need the time to set it up."

"And why is that?"

Cal looked at Branden and gave a wry smile. "Because she's Amish. An Amish lass of twenty-nine."

"Hawkins intends to marry Amish?"

Cal nodded.

Branden's eyes narrowed with an expression that said, "I think you'd better explain."

Cal pulled himself up from his seat on the bank and said, "I'll tell you this little story, but only while we work the pond. Too nice a day not to fish."

Branden agreed and followed Cal along the bank, several paces back. As they hooked and landed the day's catch, Troyer ran it all down for the professor.

"When David Hawkins first moved to Millersburg, he was a mess—Vietnam, and more. It took nearly a year, but we eventually got him straightened around. He cleaned up, forgave himself, became a member of our church, and sent for his daughter.

"For several years, things were fine. But eventually it wasn't enough. He couldn't settle in. Couldn't handle retirement. He worked for us as a janitor at the church and for me, building houses, and refused to accept a salary. He was working off a burden that had smothered his conscience—laboring as an act of contrition. It was something in his past, I can't tell you the whole story, but a quiet life in town wasn't going to be enough for him.

"Gradually, he took an interest in the Amish. He'd been fascinated with them since he moved to Millersburg, anyway. The long and the short of it is, he met a girl, fell in love, and decided to convert to Amish. A cold warrior turned Amish pacifist.

"By then we were good friends, and to tell you the truth, I thought it was an OK thing. I don't usually encourage that sort of thinking, because most Amish sects are a closed and suspicious bunch. But a life closed away from the rest of the world was the best thing for David Hawkins, if the stories he's told me are any indication. I'd never known anyone who had converted to the Amish, but I hear it happens from time to time.

"Well, eventually, like I said, Hawkins found a family that would have him, with a daughter whom they had not yet managed to marry off. Plus it was obvious that he did truly love her, and she him.

"For the past year or so, he has lived a genuine Amish life. The girl's father asked Hawkins for a two-year courtship to prove himself. Not an unwarranted precaution when you consider Hawkins's past. That was a little more than a year ago, now. In the meantime, Hawkins gave his house in town to his daughter and made plans to move out into the country."

Branden asked, "Hawkins came out of the service, and he was converting to the Amish?"

"Has converted, for all intents and purposes."

"And you can't imagine that the recent murder of his daughter will have snapped him back, hard?"

"He is a pacifist," Cal said. "He understands, completely, what that means."

"Maybe now, but he used to be a soldier," Branden argued. "And the cold-blooded murder of his daughter would have to be the harshest, rawest test of any pacifist's convictions."

"One of the roughest tests I can imagine," Cal said, "and I'm certain, beyond limit, that David Hawkins could not kill someone. Anyone. Certainly not some young reporter."

"He's killed before, evidently with great skill."

"That was a different life. David Hawkins has been made new. Plus, there's his Amish commitment to nonviolence."

"Then what was that about holding a gun to Ricky Niell's head?"

Cal sighed. "A lapse."

"And you're banking that it was only a temporary lapse," Branden said.

"I'd stake my life on it," Cal answered, eyes leveled confidently at his friend.

"So you've said. Look, Cal," Branden said, "you've got to admit. Whatever else you might say about David Hawkins, on that night in the jail, he cracked. Whatever it was that Sands told him, Hawkins cracked."

"There's nothing Sands can have told him that would send David Hawkins back to killing."

"What makes you think so, Cal?"

"Because I've measured the depth of his conversion. I know the strength of his convictions."

"Too bad Robertson doesn't know that, too."

"Indeed," Cal answered.

"I want to talk with Hawkins, Cal."

"Can't do that, Mike."

"Then let me talk with the family where he's living."

"Then you'd know where he lives."

"All right, then let's start with the girl. I've got to have something to go on, Cal," Branden argued. "According to Ricky Niell, Bruce Robertson's bound to haul you in for questioning before too much longer, and if I'm to help, you'll have to trust me a little on this."

Cal stopped beside the pond, looked down to think, and said, "Remember the high ground south of Fredericksburg where we used to camp?"

"Sure."

"The little knoll at the edge of the cliffs where we used to watch the car lights out toward Millersburg?"

"Yes."

"I'll meet you there, tomorrow, at 11:00 A.M."

"I'd like to bring Caroline."

"Fine. That'll work."

Branden thought for a moment and said, "And what do you intend to do, Cal?"

"I'll bring his fiancée—the one person who can tell you everything you need to know about David Hawkins."

6

THE next morning, after attending to business in Wayne County to the north, the Brandens drove southeast out of Wooster on Route 250 past the little roadside community of Guerne and then turned right onto the Fredericksburg road. From there, the road takes a straight course south for about seven miles through the country before it drops into a deep pocket where Fredericksburg sits at the intersection of small county roads. Those travelers who drop down into that little burg and spend enough quiet time there soon realize that they've found the old world.

Just off the northeast corner of the one main intersection there stands a little brick church with a neighborly steeple. On the southeast corner is an antique shop in a brown and tan brick building with large glass windows. A "closed" sign hangs there more often than not.

Across the street, on the southwest corner, there is a quiet, two-story, brick general store with groceries, dry goods, household items, and a short wall rack of old videos for the English to rent. In the back of the store, on worn wooden planking, an old-fashioned meat and cheese cooler stands next to a butcher's block where the local residents, mostly Amish, have their goods sliced to order and wrapped in white or brown butcher's paper. Out back is an ample lot for horses and buggies, where, on most days, an assortment of rigs will be hitched at the rail.

The Brandens stopped at the blinking yellow light, waited for a buggy to clear the intersection, and then began the long, slow climb up the steep hill out of Fredericksburg. The road climbed south and wound its way over the hills into Holmes County. For the second day in a row, the sun was out strong in an astonishing aqua sky. A forecaster on Cleveland radio had read the pattern of winds aloft, and was calling for a clear and windless day, highs in the upper seventies.

After several miles, the Brandens turned onto a small gravel lane that disappeared into a stand of timber near a wooded stream. The road meandered with the stream and then carried them over the water on a bridge of wooden planks. As the stream fell away into a long valley of Amish farms to their left, the Brandens skirted high on the right, along the west rim. They passed large Amish houses and barns, Daadihauses, grape arbors, and watering troughs. Windmills stood idle against the sky amid fields of crops newly planted.

They passed a one-room schoolhouse with a woodshed. Behind the little school, there were two outhouses, and an old merry-go-round tilting wildly at an angle on its rusty center post. There was a softball diamond with a new backstop.

An engine shop and a family sawmill came up on the left, and then a little cemetery stood quietly on the right, with white head-stones in tall grass. A wagonload of kids, drawn by two slug-gish Haflingers, came along the road from the other direction.

Eventually the road leveled out onto a wide, high plateau planted luxuriantly with spring crops. Iron-wheeled farm ma-chines stood along the fences, motionless without their teams. In the distance, an Amish farmer in a straw hat stood atop a boxy red manure spreader, working his way through a fallow field behind a pair of draft horses.

Branden turned off the lane and followed a worn path of weed-choked gravel across a field of winter wheat. The little path looped back behind an oil pumper and came to an end at the southernmost edge of the high plateau. The view, at three points of the compass, carried the eyes to at least four counties.

Caroline stood beside their small sedan in the delicate, knee-high winter wheat and took in the panoramic vista. To her right, about two hundred yards farther west on the plateau, there was a tall red barn and a two-story white frame house, perched near the rim with a view into the west. Straight ahead, on a distant hill, she recognized the curves of Route 83 as it turned into Millersburg. To her left, she saw the receding hills in the east, where the miniature smokestacks of a plant near Massillon put a round puff of white against the horizon.

"This is the same field you brought me to that summer during graduate school when I came here to visit you," Caroline said, smiling nostalgically.

"It's a special place," Branden said.

"Because of you and Cal."

"Because of you," Branden said. "But yes, because of me and Cal and Bruce Robertson. These were our summer camping grounds."

"Boys," Caroline remarked. "If I remember, you just happened to have a blanket with you the afternoon we came here."

The professor grinned boyishly, remembering the slow, tender afternoon that had sealed their commitment to one another. He drew her to him and kissed her.

Caroline held him close for a moment and then released him. "You three used to come up here to camp," Caroline said. "When did that start?"

"Seventh grade, I think," he said. "We came out here on a whim one weekend. Built a little campfire and made ourselves sick smoking cigars. At least Cal and I got sick. Bruce liked it from the start."

"So you're responsible for Bruce's smoking, Professor."

Branden made a wry expression and defended himself. "Bruce didn't smoke at all in high school. He started in the army, Caroline."

Caroline waved her hand dismissively, pronouncing her husband guilty as charged.

"That was just the first time, Caroline. With the smoking. After that, we came up here any time we could, and no more cigars!"

The professor saw he was wasting his breath, so he ambled over to the fence line at the edge of the drop-off. He walked a short length of the fence with his eyes down, doubled back a few paces, and motioned Caroline to his side. He began pulling up weeds to reveal a ring of large stones. "Our campfire ring is still here," he said. "We got permission from the old Dutchman who owned the field, and we kept a permanent site here. We'd use it mainly on weekends. Holidays too. Sometimes we brought shotguns and threw clay pigeons for each other out over the drop-off. Sometimes we'd shoot quail and roast them for supper."

Caroline frowned, teasing him with her disapproval.

"We didn't do that very often," Branden said. "Mostly we'd hike the creek bottoms down below. There's a bass pond down there in the tangles, and we'd fish for our dinner. At night, Bruce would go down with his gig and catch bullfrogs."

"I guess you're going to tell me you ate frog legs, too," Caroline sighed.

"Delicious," Branden said emphatically. He kicked at the blackened earth in the campfire ring and said, "The last time we came up here was the night before Bruce went off to basic training." He gazed into the distance, dwelling on memories. Eventually he said, "It hasn't changed up here in all those years. No electricity anywhere."

Caroline looked in every direction and could not find a single electric wire.

In all, they waited there for more than an hour. On the little gravel lane where they had made their turn into the field, an occasional buggy rolled slowly into view and then went down out of sight toward the valley beyond. One buggy rolled by twice and then came along a third time with all of its black window flaps tied down. It seemed to tarry briefly at the little grassy path to the oil pumper, and then its black iron wheels wobbled away in the gravel. In a few moments, the buggy reappeared at the white house on the western edge of the plateau. It turned around in the oval driveway in front of the house and then came slowly back to the path. This time, after hesitating again at the path, the driver pulled hard on the reins, tapped the buggy whip off the horse's flank, and pulled the buggy onto the path through the field.

The Brandens watched it approach through the wheat. When it stopped beside their car, all of the window flaps remained closed. The only windows were small rectangular holes, about two inches by four inches, in the top center of the flaps. They waited beside their car and heard soft, unhurried voices speaking Low German. Branden recognized Cal Troyer's voice, muffled behind the black flaps. The other voice was a woman's. After a while, the windshield flap on the buggy was rolled up, and there sat Cal Troyer on the left, next to a young Amish woman in traditional dress.

Her leather shoes were the old, black lace-up kind. Her ankles showed only an inch of black hose. Her light plum dress was altogether plain. She wore a long black shawl over her shoulders, and it was clasped in front by a pin. The collar of her dress came up high around her neck, and her large black bonnet lapped down to her shoulders on the sides and back, entirely covering her hair and neck. It also was tied closely against her cheeks to cover her ears. Her hands were sturdy, folded delicately in her lap. Her face was a tranquil white, eyes a soft brown behind plain, round, wire-rimmed spectacles.

Branden pushed away from his spot leaning against the car

and walked over to the left side of the buggy, next to Cal. He took off his wide-brimmed black Amish hat and ran fingers through his hair.

Cal set the hand brake on the buggy and said, "Frauline Raber, I'd like you to meet Herr Professor Doctor Michael Branden." Then he turned farther toward her on the seat and added, "He's a professor of Civil War history at Millersburg College. Mike, this is Abigail Raber."

The Amish woman turned slightly toward Branden and, with a reserve that bordered on painful shyness, she tipped her head an inch in greeting and said, "Herr Professor."

He stood at the left front corner of the buggy and wordlessly nodded in return. As she faced him, he held her eyes, and before she had turned away, he saw an unpretentious Dutch beauty in her features. A simple and delicate tenderness. Large, gentle eyes that gave her an aloof, almost alluring air of detachment from the world. Full lips and a long, arching scar that started under her chin and curved along her right jaw, up under the flaps of her bonnet toward her right ear.

Abigail's eyes fell to her hands in her lap, and then she looked back into the professor's eyes and said, "Pastor Troyer has advised me that I should tell you about Mr. Hawkins." Her eyes peered into his for more than a proper length of time, and she seemed to take the measure of his heart.

Branden answered, "Yes. If you are willing."

She drew her eyes away from the professor. "We are to be married."

Branden held back a discrete moment and then encouraged her with, "I understand he's a most remarkable man."

She considered that briefly with a skeptical expression and said, "I'm not sure about remarkable, Herr Professor. I would say, rather, that he is capable. Maybe, also, uncommon. The most uncommon and capable man I could ever have met."

Her candor startled him. She looked at him with an intense,

peaceful calm. There was a momentary, glintering sheen in her eyes. With a disarming gratitude, she whispered, "He has rescued me."

Branden glanced for a moment to Cal, and then he held out his hand and asked, "Would you like to walk a spell, Miss Raber?"

Abigail gathered up the folds of her dress, climbed forward in the buggy past Cal, took the professor's hand, and stepped down and off the rig. The buggy rocked on its springs, and the horse pranced against the brake. Cal steadied it with the reins.

Branden introduced Abigail to Caroline, then turned and strolled with Abigail several dozen yards through the winter wheat, until they reached the southern precipice. Her black and plum outfit swayed against the tender green hues of the new wheat. As they approached an old fence line, a dozen or so quail bolted out of the rough and thundered on wing into the sky.

They stood together at the fence line, perched high over a long and distant view, and she spoke to him softly of David Hawkins. She told of his fervor to study the Amish ways. Told of his extraordinary determination to master the plain life. Told of the early days, almost four years ago, when he first had showed up at a Sunday service, in Deacon Yoder's barns. He had sat quietly, head down, among the men. Like no man she had ever known, he had gazed exclusively into her eyes when she had helped the other women serve dinner to the men on the kitchen benches after the services.

She reached up and lightly ran a finger along the scar on her cheek and told how David Hawkins had labored in the fields of her father. How he had come to her one evening at the well beside the houses. He had pumped the water and sought her eyes. Held her hand and began to court her openly.

Finally, she told of the evening over a year ago when he had proposed to her. They had driven an open buggy out through the fields, and although he had never asked her about it, she had told him of the horse that had kicked in her face when she was only twelve. And she had cried beside Hawkins on the buckboard, telling this one, most uncommon man, for the first time, of the lonely, inward, hidden vigil she had kept over the years because of her deformity. Last, she told the professor how Hawkins had softened in that miraculous moment and had wept inconsolably in her arms, broken, beseeching her to understand, as he had confessed to her the dark things he had done in the world.

As Abigail finished, she turned to look back at the buggy where Cal and Caroline waited. Her eyes swept over the high plateau and then into the valley. She looked at Professor Branden, into his eyes. She considered, as she stood there with him, why she had confided so completely in an Englisher. She wondered what events she might set in motion when she decided to trust him. Tried to understand why she had found him so easy to talk to, and realized that she had already committed herself to trusting him unreservedly. Then, in a clear moment of honesty, she conceded to herself that she, and David Hawkins, needed helping.

They were to be married. Father had promised her hand. But only after a two-year courtship. David had done so well. His conversion was real; she knew that with a lover's assurance. Knew it in her soul, where words were inadequate to express her deepest thoughts. She knew it in her prayers, where the Spirit spoke to her, spoke for her, spoke for them. And she knew it because of the irrevocable promises of the most uncommon man she had ever known. Because of the promises of the only man who had understood her. Because of the word of the man who had rescued her from a sure fate in her closed society.

But Abigail Raber also understood that the murder of David Hawkins's English daughter had changed him. And she admitted to herself, as she stood next to Branden, that the night at the jail had produced a crisis for Hawkins, a crisis of faith that would test David Hawkins to the breaking point. The words that the murderer had spoken to him had hit like a hammer against an anvil and threatened to pound David Hawkins out of her life. To shatter the new faith that he had found. She knew it, now, with a clear and consuming certainty. The words and deeds of the murderer of his daughter could push David Hawkins out of her reach forever. Could destroy the life they had intended to build. Could drop her back into the closed society where unmarried women grew old to a spinster's fate. Could drive Hawkins to an unforgivable deed. To an act of revenge that her father would never accept. Drive him to vengeance in a community where vengeance was forbidden. Drive him out of her life forever, away from the faith she could never abandon.

All of these thoughts grew in Abigail to a desperate but still tender realization that her future and David Hawkins's future depended on the decisions she was making there on the high plateau. Without actually thinking the precise words, and without actually coming to a recognizable moment when she had found her resolve, Abigail Raber held out her trust to Michael Branden.

She turned to Branden, eyes glistening, with an expression of calm and unfaltering certainty, and said, "Pastor Troyer has said that you can help us. We know that there has been another murder. We also know that the sheriff believes David has done it.

"But I know, Professor, that David cannot have done this. I also know, full well, who he was, and what he had done, before he came to me. But, Herr Professor, David Hawkins is a new man. I saw his baptism. I heard his vows. I know his heart."

"It would help," Branden said, "if I could speak with him." For a lingering moment, she seemed to gather herself to a task. Then she said, almost inaudibly, "We do not know where David Hawkins is."

Slowly she turned and started back toward her buggy. Branden followed silently. At the back of her buggy, she reached in under some blankets and pulled out a heavy object. When she turned around, she was holding a Ruger .22 automatic pistol by the tip of the barrel, the heavy gun hanging from her fingertips. Branden looped his little finger through the trigger guard and took it from her gingerly. She turned and drew out another piece, a long black metal tube, threaded on one end, which Branden recognized as a silencer. He asked Caroline for a handkerchief and took possession of the silencer.

As he stood holding the two pieces at the back of her buggy, Abigail said, "We haven't seen anything of Mr. Hawkins since last Wednesday, when I found these wrapped in some blankets in his buggy."

7

Monday, June 9
1:45 P.M.

BEFORE driving Abigail back to the Raber homestead, Cal Troyer drew Branden a map locating the Raber farm in the hills east of Fredericksburg. Cal handed Abigail up into the buggy, climbed into the driver's seat, and turned the horse back down the narrow path. The Brandens drove south to Millersburg, lunched together on their back porch, and talked their way through all of the larger and finer details of the case.

In the afternoon, Branden drove down off the college hills to the center of town and found a parking spot at the bank behind the red brick jail. He walked up Clay Street, turned at the courthouse lawn, and pulled open the front door to the jail.

Inside on his left, a wooden bench for visitors and a soft-drink machine stood next to a black iron door that gave access to the first-floor gang cell. On his right, there was a long wooden counter with a swinging door at its far end. Behind the counter, a desk stacked with an odd collection of old and new radio equipment crowded another desk where Ellie Troyer sat typing. Branden went up to the counter, rested his elbows on it, and waited without speaking.

Ellie sat with her back to him. She continued typing steadily, saying merely, "Yes?" without looking up from the keys.

Branden said nothing.

She turned around from her typing, grinned at him, shook her head, turned back to the typewriter, finished a line on a form, pulled the form through the rollers, and tossed it into her out-box. Without saying anything more to Branden, she wheeled her chair around to face the intercom, pushed the button marked "Bruce," and caroled, "Oh, Sheriff." in a singsong tone.

They heard a gruff "Yes?" through the static of the old intercom.

"We've got someone here who can help you with those little college problems you've been grumbling about."

"Who's that?"

"Come and see for yourself."

At the end of Ellie's counter, where the swinging door cuts through, the hall into the rest of the old jailhouse leads straight back to the rear door. Off that hallway on the right, the first door leads to the sheriff's big office on the northwest corner of the building, and a squad room is further along the hall. On the left are two interview rooms. The sheriff's office has windows looking out onto both Clay Street to the west and Courthouse Square to the north. The office also shares one wall with Ellie Troyer's alcove out front. After a brief delay, Ellie and Branden heard the door to Robertson's office open, and presently he appeared at the front counter, lumbering along slowly as he read a typed page.

When he saw it was Mike Branden at the counter, he tossed the page into Ellie's in-box, held out his hand from behind the counter, smiled, grinned, and then laughed and said, "Well I declare. It's moldy Doc Branden come down off his hill."

He tapped at Ellie's chair with the edge of his leather sole, glanced at her mischievously, and added in a loud whisper, "They don't let him out for summer until he's handed in all of his grades."

Branden shook Robertson's hand, held on to it firmly, and

pulled the big sheriff out across the counter. Robertson sent the professor a challenging schoolboy look, laughed, and then faked a panic tone. "Help me, Ellie darlin'."

Ellie shook her head at them both and sat back unconcerned.

Branden released Robertson's hand, laughing. Robertson reached around Ellie to her coffeepot and filled two Styrofoam cups. He handed one over the counter to Branden, sipped on his, and asked, "You want to tell me what in heaven's name is going on up at that college of yours, Mike?"

"Nothing out of the ordinary, so far as I know," Branden answered, instantly on guard.

"Oh, is that a fact?" Robertson said and then, "Tell him, Ellie."

"You tell him yourself, Sheriff. You're the one's been hollering most about it."

Robertson set his coffee on the counter, reached into his shirt pocket and lit a Winston. He drew on it vigorously, blew out smoke, and laid the Winston in an ashtray. He was tall, broad, and round. His fingers were disproportionately big, and his hands were almost double the size of most. His neck puffed out over his collar. His pleasant round face gave him a look many people mistook for carefree jolliness, but his eyes were sharp steel blue. His gray hair was cut closer than fashionable, in a flattop. Today his tie was still in place—unusual, Branden noted, for his intense, irascible friend.

Branden knew how Robertson worked. He'd lumber into his office with a local miscreant, sprawl casually in his chair, light a smoke, undo his tie, and lull some unsuspecting soul into mistaking his jolly size for evidence of a simpleton's stupidity. Anyone who knew Robertson well could attest that the incisive traps he laid in interviews could be detected only by watching his eyes.

Branden sipped at his coffee, and winked at Ellie with his standard, unconcerned "Oh, Bruce, come now" expression.

Then to Robertson he said, "You've got a problem with our little college?"

Robertson held his cigarette to his lips, closed his eyes slightly, drew on it, and trickled smoke as he talked. "My sister does," he said. "Her kid goes to your college. He wants to be a doctor. Science, math, biology. But his adviser says there's plenty of time to pursue a professional career. Do that later, he says. Sample the whole college to start with, and then get going on the sciences when he's sure that's what he really wants to do.

"Trouble is, if they don't get started on the sciences right away, the prerequisites make it impossible to graduate in four years. So I've got a nephew who's just figured out that he's pretty much on the five-year plan."

Branden rubbed at his temples and said, "Sounds a bit out of the ordinary." He looked to Ellie for help, but she shared Robertson's skeptical expression.

"All right, I'll see what I can do," Branden said in surrender. "This is Shirley's boy Joe, right? See if you can get his adviser's name."

The sheriff nodded as Branden finished his coffee in a large gulp. He tossed the light Styrofoam cup toward the round black can in Ellie's corner, and missed. As Robertson watched Ellie rebound for Branden, the professor changed the subject. "Bruce, I'm here because of Cal Troyer."

Robertson looked sternly at the professor and stubbed out his cigarette. He loosened his tie, unbuttoned his collar, rubbed at a chafed spot on his neck, swung the counter door back, and led Branden down the hall to his office.

Inside, a massive cherry desk stood in front of the south wall where bookshelves ran floor to ceiling and wall to wall. The bookshelves held everything from knickknacks and law books to a tape player. Prominent among the assorted items was a matching set of several dozen red and tan Zane Grey novels.

On the west wall, two large windows overlooked Clay Street.

The windows were open, and the roar of a diesel tour bus, stopped at the traffic light, mixed with the noise of a few passing cars and an occasional horn. The north wall had two matching windows overlooking the Civil War monument on the courthouse lawn. The east wall was split by the door into Robertson's office. One short length of this east wall, nearest Robertson's desk, displayed an irregular collection of a hundred or so police department arm patches, tacked randomly to the old pine paneling. Against the other section of the east wall, the one that backed against Ellie Troyer's front counter, a low credenza held a coffee maker and several cans, filters, and mugs. Robertson eased into the swivel chair behind his cherry desk and clasped his fingers over his belt. Branden moved to the west windows and looked out at the traffic on Clay Street.

Directly, Robertson said, "Does Cal Troyer know I'm looking for David Hawkins?"

Branden answered plainly, "Yes."

"You told him yourself?"

"Yesterday," Branden said, turning to Robertson.

"Then, can you tell me where he is?"

Branden reached casually into his front jeans pocket, felt the folded map that Cal had drawn of the Raber farms, and said, "I don't know where he is. It's not likely that I'll see him in the next day or two, either."

"Can you tell Cal that I need his help with the bishops? Or his help directly, if he can locate Hawkins." Robertson was still slouched in his chair, now leaning back with his fingers locked behind his head, giving his neck a swollen look. Only his eyes moved, following as Branden stepped to the north windows. The professor looked idly across the lawn to the statue of a Union soldier and turned to face Robertson again.

"Cal doesn't know where David Hawkins is, Bruce."

"Do you know that Hawkins is my most likely suspect in the murder of Eric Bromfield?" Robertson asked brusquely.

"Bruce, you've taken a wrong tack on this."

"We've done a lot of checking. He was Special Forces, Mike, and he's evidently disappeared after talking in the jail one night with Jesse Sands. If nothing else, he could be planning to kill Sands for murdering his daughter," Robertson said. His eyes were narrowed and confident.

"Then tell me how you figure that," Branden said, skeptical.

"Don't toy with me, Mike," Robertson said. "We've got two murders here, and I speculate we'll have a third before it's all over."

"You found the Bromfield kid, Bruce," Branden said.

"So?"

"So, a pro like Hawkins would not have left a loose end like that. It only points suspicion toward him, and I doubt he'd want to do that."

Robertson nodded agreement and said, "Maybe he wanted Bromfield found."

"I hope you've got other suspects," Branden said.

"I don't at this time," Robertson complained. "I want Hawkins brought in, and I'm prepared to do everything possible to accomplish that, Mike. If for nothing else, so he can't make a run at Jesse Sands."

Branden pulled up a straight wooden chair in front of Robertson's old desk and said, "Tell me what you know."

Robertson rolled his swivel chair forward, propped the soles of his shoes on the casters of his chair, and leaned toward Branden with his forearms on his desk.

"It's the whole pattern," Robertson said. "Janet Hawkins murdered by Jesse Sands."

Branden waved him on.

Robertson kept at it. "Next, we've got the Bromfield murder. We get to nosing around and Marty Holcombe tells us that Bromfield had done a little research. Found out that Hawkins was the sort of guy who wouldn't want it known what he had been doing for a living. The same fella who came to my jail one night to forgive Jesse Sands. By the way, Sands's lawyer has been screaming bloody murder since then about our violating his client's civil rights. Plans to drag us into court."

Branden said, "Hawkins had Sands by the throat. Don't you think he would have killed Sands then and there if he were going to?"

"And get away how?" Robertson asked.

"He evidently didn't have any trouble taking care of Ricky Niell."

Robertson grimaced.

Branden said, "How does this all add up to three murders?"

"Hawkins was Army, Special Forces."

"So?"

"So," Robertson said, "I figure Hawkins is planning to make another run at Sands. Come back and finish what Ricky stopped him from doing that night at the jail." Before Branden could object, he held up a hand and added, "I've got something that you don't know."

"And that is?"

"This morning in the jail, Jesse Sands started laughing. Danced in his cell upstairs like a drunken fool. The deputies came and got me, and when I got to Sands, he had calmed down some. Just stood in his cell, grinning out at me like he'd won the lottery. Looked like an idiot, too.

"Then he started taunting us through the bars. Said, 'You country clods'll never figure it out. You'll never get him in time. I've got him, and you fools'll never see it coming.' You know, Mike, the old 'You don't get it now, and you never will' sort of thing. I stood there for a while, staring in at him through the bars, and then asked, 'Get what?'"

"He walked to the back of his cell and tapped on the glass over his window. That's bulletproof glass on the inside, bars in the middle, and then another pane of glass on the outside. There was a rectangle of paper taped to the outside glass, with writing on it facing in so Sands could read it."

Robertson slid the center drawer of his desk open and pulled out a rectangle of white poster board, about five inches by eight inches. He handed it to Branden, and Branden read it. Then he read it again.

Eventually Branden asked, "And you think this means that David Hawkins will kill Sands for the murder of his daughter?"

"No doubt in my mind."

"This could mean any number of things, Bruce."

"I'll tell you what it means, Mike. It means we've got a squirrelly Vietnam vet running loose in Holmes County, and when we take Sands out of that cell, maybe to court, maybe to a doctor —anywhere, Mike, anywhere at all—then Hawkins is going to make his run at Sands, and if Hawkins is still as good as they say he was, Sands will take a bullet, just like Eric Bromfield did."

"Cal would say you're wrong, Bruce, and based on what I've learned about David Hawkins, I'm inclined to agree with him," Branden said.

"I need to talk with Hawkins. Cal Troyer at the very least," Robertson said flatly.

Branden stood up, tossed the sign onto Robertson's desk, said "If I see Cal, I'll tell him you're looking for him," and strolled out of the office, endeavoring to appear unconcerned.

Robertson watched him go, lit another Winston, picked up the sign, and read the block letters again:

IT IS MINE TO AVENGE
I WILL REPAY

Then he tossed the placard back into his center drawer and sat back with his cigarette to think.

After a few minutes, Branden strolled back into the sheriff's office with a brown grocery bag. He set it gingerly on the sheriff's desk and used his handkerchief to draw out the pistol and silencer that Abigail Raber had given him. In a challenging tone he said, "Here's a little puzzle for you, Sheriff. If you can prove this is the gun that killed Bromfield, I'll tell you where I got it."

8

Monday, June 9
6:30 P.M.

CAROLINE served dinner that night on their large, curly maple kitchen table, a gift from Bishop Eli Miller and his family in appreciation of the Brandens' help the previous summer. The Brandens talked again about Abigail Raber and David Hawkins. About Cal Troyer and Bruce Robertson. About Marty Holcombe and his murdered reporter, Eric Bromfield. About Jesse Sands and the note stuck to the outside of his jail cell window.

Toward sunset, Branden ducked into the garage, loaded gear into the bed of their pickup, covered it all with a blue tarp, and tied it down. When it was secure, he called into the house from the door to the garage, made an excuse about a brief errand, and drove to a small shop where he picked out an extravagant bottle of wine and several boxes of crackers, some cheese, and a jar of peanut butter. When he returned to their house on the circle near the college, he left the truck out on the street with the motor running, bounded into the house, led Caroline out playfully, locked up, and drove them out to the high plateau where they had been earlier that day.

In an out-of-the-way corner of the high field of winter wheat, he spread a ground cloth, a double-wide sleeping bag, pillows, glasses, wine, and snacks. Caroline sat blushing in the cab of the truck and watched with embarrassed amazement. He looked over his handiwork, smiled his approval, stepped to her door, and opened it with a ceremonial bow.

She wrapped her arms tightly over her seat belt, blushed extravagantly, and said, "And just what do you expect me to do, Professor Branden?"

He tickled her on a spot he knew along her collar bone, slipped her seat belt loose when she laughed, and pulled her out of the cab into his arms. "I expect you, Mrs. Branden, to enjoy the sunset."

As the sun fell, the clear sky quickly released the heat of the day, and they soon eased themselves into the sleeping bag. The sun grew majestically larger as it set and then lingered on the horizon. There was a delicate, expanding, golden-orange hue along the horizon and then a blazing rose, tinged with a flickering deep red. They slid deeper into the sleeping bag as a gentle breeze began to stir over the plateau.

Later, the stars came out, and they lay under the sky's sparkling canopy. Long into the night, as the stars made their circuit around, she fell asleep in his arms. He rolled onto his back, eased his arm under her head, drew her close, and lay gazing up at the glittering sky.

In time, the troubles of the day found him there and would not set him free. He turned them inside-out and upside-down in his mind. He looked them over from every new angle he could find. He thought the puzzle through from every direction.

Cal had every reason to stand by Hawkins and defend him. And until Hawkins actually did something, up until the very moment when he might precipitate a crisis, Cal would be right about David Hawkins. Trouble was, Bruce Robertson was also right. David Hawkins was, if nothing else, certainly a loose wire. To Robertson he seemed a reasonable suspect in the murder of Eric Bromfield. He was probably also gunning for Jesse Sands. Then there was Abigail Raber, caught up, more than anyone, in the crisis of Hawkins's dilemma.

In his mind, Branden saw her again, tall and thin at the edge of the field, a rare, deep beauty in her eyes, a cruel scar along her delicate cheek. He remembered her long Amish dress, her black bonnet and shawl. The way her fingers had held her shawl clasped against her breast. The way she had spoken softly of her hope and faith in David Hawkins, as she had gazed peacefully into the distance.

It was Abigail whose destiny now lay in the hands of a re-formed soldier. Abigail whose love had been pledged to a man who now surely was making the decisions of a lifetime. Abigail who had told Branden on this high plateau that she had placed her future's hope into the hands of the most uncommon man she had ever known. And it was Abigail, Branden realized, who had convinced him, even more than Cal had, of the faith and honor of David Hawkins.

9

Tuesday, June 10
4:30 A.M.

THE habit of a lifetime found Abigail Raber awake before
dawn. She dressed quietly by the light of a kerosene lamp, carried the lamp from the little Daadihaus into the big house, and
set it on the kitchen counter, next to the massive, silver and
black, wood cooking stove. She gathered several kindling sticks
from the woodbox, opened the iron door to the front of the
stove, encouraged the flames to life from coals, added more
wood, and softly closed the heavy door. From a cupboard overhead she collected two cups and two saucers. From the icebox,
she took a tiny pitcher of whole cream. She poured water into
a teakettle from a large counter pitcher she had filled at the hand
pump the night before, and placed the kettle on one of the round
heat plates atop the stove. As the water heated, she warmed
herself by the stove. When her tea was ready, she poured in a
splash of cream, stirred it with a small silver spoon, and sat down
on a plain wooden bench at the large kitchen table for her
morning devotions.

As had long been his custom, Abigail's father soon joined
her there. She closed her scriptures, made tea for him, and they
sat together in the light of the kerosene lamp, talking quietly as
they had done for years.

"Abi," he said at length. "He will make you decide. If your
David will not come home to you, you must let him go."

"I cannot, Father. He is the only one I'll ever have. You know that. He is the only one I'll ever be able to love. The only one who will ever love me."

"Abi. Herr Hawkins es der Hoche. He is a high one. After only a year with us, can you expect more of him than this?"

"He is one of us, Father. You saw him take the vows."

"If he chooses the wrong path now, his vows will have meant nothing. Not to us. Not to God."

"He will choose us, I know it."

Tears flooded her eyes, and her father drew near and embraced her briefly, somewhat embarrassed. "Abi. Listen to me. He was a warrior. He will take a warrior's revenge for his daughter. There's nothing else for him."

"He can be forgiven."

"No, Abi. Sel ist net recht. You know that is not right."

"I love him, Father. Only you have known how much I do truly love him."

"Versteh, Abi. Versteh. I understand well enough. But revenge is a crushing thing. A burden that will eat away at him forever. It will destroy him. Eventually, it will destroy his ability to love you. Destroy his ability even to care for you. To show a father's love to your children. If he avenges himself now, you'll never be free of it. You know this, Abi. It is our creed. God has forbidden us to avenge ourselves on any man. Abi, it is our way. Vengeance destroys the avenger above all."

10

Tuesday, June 10
8:15 A.M.

AS daylight crept out atop the hills, the professor drove Caroline home. After breakfast, he appeared at the jail. The deputies lounging in the squad room at the rear of the jail reported that the sheriff could be found at Chester's barbershop around the corner, and they joked among themselves about the pleasant few moments of peace that had fallen upon the jail in his absence. Branden got permission to leave his truck in one of the spots for cruisers behind the jail and walked the two short blocks to Chester's.

It was an old barbershop in a ground-floor location, fronted with a tall picture window. The barber's pole that hung over the sidewalk had stopped turning years ago, but the regulars knew when Chester would be open. The regulars knew, and the others didn't much matter to Chester. Branden found Robertson inside, leaning back in the second chair, taking a shave.

Chester had once had a partner, but he had quit several years back, and now the first chair was piled high with an erratic stack of *Field and Stream, Outdoor Life,* and *Lions International.* There were a half dozen old wooden chairs backed up against the window in front, and, on the low windowsill, there were more old magazines and a faded cardboard display for hair creams. Chester had never paid much attention to housekeeping, and the only things not dusty in his shop were the shiny red plastic seat cushions, where customers' pants had done the polishing for him. Branden took a seat against the window and waited.

As Branden turned the pages of a worn *National Geographic,* a young boy was brought in by his mother. She put him into a chair by the window and spoke a few words to Chester about the haircut that she wanted for her son. She paid in advance and reminded the boy to come straight down the street to the bank when he was finished. The little fellow muttered something inaudible to her, and blushed furiously red when she bent to kiss him.

Once she had left, Branden eased forward in his chair, caught Chester's eye, nodded toward the boy, and winked. Branden leaned over toward the boy, said, "I see your mom brought you in," and glanced back at Robertson to get the sheriff's attention.

"Your mom brought you in," Branden continued, "but I'm willing to bet you're old enough for a grown-up cut today," and then added, "He is, Chester, I swear. Take a look, man."

Chester strolled out from behind the barber's chair, looked the kid over, gave a little skeptical snort, and said, "Can't be sure, Doc."

"I know he is, Chester." To the boy, Branden said, "Look son, it seems to me you're as ready as you'll ever be. For a regular cut, that is."

"Professor," Chester said officiously, "You need to remember the last time you were wrong about one of these pink laddies."

"I'm not a pink laddie," the boy asserted sternly.

"You see, Chester. I told you. He's ready. Aren't you son?"

"I'm not a pink laddie."

By now Robertson had put a stop to his shave. He stepped down out of the barber's chair, shook hair off the apron that hung from his sizable neck, and winked at the professor. He held out his enormous hand to help the boy up into the tall barber's chair, and said, "Well, then, you step on up here, young man."

Chester pumped the seat high, threw a striped apron around the boy's neck, spread it out over his lap, and started snapping his hand shears near the lad's ears.

Robertson leaned over a bit, apron hanging down in front of his belly. He propped his hands on his knees, and stared the boy straight into his eyes. "Good decision, lad. Now pay attention."

The boy's head turned to the clipping sound of the scissors behind his ear, and Robertson pulled him by the chin back around to face toward the front. "Now, young fella," he said, "the best part is the first. Just a normal haircut."

"Sheriff, are you sure about this?" Chester said with exaggerated concern.

Robertson looked deeply into the boy's eyes and asked, "You're sure, aren't you boy?"

From his chair, Branden said, "Of course he's sure," and only just managed to keep a smile off his face.

The little fella nodded weakly and tried to read some comfort in the big sheriff's eyes.

Robertson gestured with confidence and said, "He's quite certain, Chester," and Chester began to snip out the very style of haircut that the boy's mother had earlier described.

Robertson continued to stand directly in front of the barber chair, watching intently as Chester made a show of clipping. The sheriff's legs straddled the footrest and his hands were planted on the armrests near the boy's hands. His apron hung low in front, and he was nose to nose with the boy, five inches off. Half his face was still lathered, and he used the end of the barber's apron to wipe off the remaining foam.

"Now, the next part is really not so bad," Robertson said. "You've probably heard some bad things, but that's all exaggeration. We've got a styptic pencil in case you bleed, and even if you do, it'll probably be only this once. Nobody bleeds much after the first one."

The boy's eyes widened into saucers, and Chester began to strop a straight razor slowly back and forth along a leather strap attached to the barber chair. The boy squirmed and eyed the razor wildly. Robertson laid a hand on his knee to calm him. "Steady now," he said. "This probably won't be too bad at all."

Branden stood, arms folded, to assess the boy's courage.

Chester ran some hot water into a lather cup and beat it to a froth with a shaving brush so that the boy could watch. While it was still warm, he slapped it lavishly on the boy's neck behind each ear. The kid jerked practically out of his seat in surprise, and Robertson eased him back into the barber chair with a confident hand.

Chester took one last pass over the strop and flipped the knife edge of the razor to give it a little tinging sound as it lifted off the leather. Then Chester silently turned the straight razor over to use the rounded back edge, and laid the cold, dull steel against the boy's neck behind the ear.

"Hold it one second, Chester," Robertson said. "It's a man's cut, son. You sure you're ready?"

The lad swallowed hard, looked around the room and back to Robertson. He was obviously considering bolting for the door, but fought the impulse bravely, and nodded weakly "Yes."

"Now don't move a muscle," Robertson warned and then gave the go-ahead to Chester.

The boy closed his eyes tightly, and Chester slowly drew the dull edge down along the boy's neck behind the ear, scraping off lather. The kid rose six inches out of his chair, opened his eyes wide, and nearly fainted.

Robertson smiled encouragement to the lad and said, "Halfway done."

Chester walked around to the other side of the chair, laid the dull steel against the boy's neck again, lifted up the ear, and drew the back of the razor slowly down through the lather. When he was finished with the second stroke, Chester took a warm towel, wiped excess lather off the boy's neck, and dabbed at a little patch of white on his ear.

"Now the last part," Robertson said. The lad stared back at the sheriff, unable to speak.

"Mennen or Jarvis, Chester?" Branden asked, and moved in closer.

"Jarvis, I think, Doc. Jarvis is his brand all the way."

"You agree, son?"

The boy nodded his head the slightest fraction of a terrified inch.

"Jarvis," Robertson announced, and Chester poured some out, slapped it into his palms, said "This might sting a bit," and clamped both of his cold hands to the sides of the lad's neck.

The aroma came suddenly into the boy's nostrils and he choked a bit. When he opened his eyes, he saw Robertson standing back from the front of the chair, giving the thumbs-up sign with both hands.

The boy smiled and wrestled himself into a taller position on the barber's chair. He glanced around the room, looked back at Chester, and smiled a little bit more. When he realized he wouldn't die in the barber's chair, he smiled wider still.

They let him sit there a little while and celebrate his victory. When they were sure he'd be steady on his feet, they saw him to the door, shook his little hand, congratulated him exuberantly, and sent him on his way some six inches taller. Branden returned to his seat, unable to force the smile from his face. "Bruce," he said, "if word gets out about us, the mothers in this town will have us locked away."

"Now what would you suppose he's talking about, Chester?" Robertson said and sat back in the chair to finish his shave.

"Wouldn't know, Sheriff," Chester said and lathered the sheriff's face again.

Branden laughed outright and said, "The next time that kid comes in for a haircut, he'll likely not let his mother through the door. And he'll ask for Jarvis."

"You bet," Chester agreed.

"And he'll ask for a manly cut and shave for years to come," Robertson said. "Then along about ten years from now, Chester here'll actually start using the sharp edge on that razor. The way I see it, we did the kid a favor."

Branden chuckled, clasped his hands behind his head, and stretched his legs out straight, ankles crossed. Chester finished up, Robertson paid, and Branden walked with the sheriff back toward the jail.

"Bruce, I want you to give me some time to find David Hawkins," Branden said, as they came abreast of the old red jail.

"Can't do that, Mike. Sands is due in court in a little over a week, and that'll pretty much be the end of things."

Branden stopped on the lawn, considering how best to reason with his old friend.

"You've got to think about this like razors, Bruce," he said.

Robertson eyed him skeptically.

"Bromfield was killed by a dull razor. Hawkins is the sharp razor. Special Forces. The best. He'd never have left Bromfield out where his body could be found so readily."

Robertson said, "That may be all well and good, but I've got to assume that Hawkins is a wrong kind of guy."

"If you ease off on hunting him down, you'll probably find he comes in on his own one day."

"I can't afford to wait and see, Mike."

Branden stared down thoughtfully at his sandals. "Have you done the ballistics on that pistol yet?"

Robertson said, "The .22 bullets that killed Bromfield were high velocity, and they broke up in his skull, so we can't match the rifling in the barrel. Coroner's still got some connections with the labs in Cleveland, though, and we expect we can match powder residue on Bromfield's temple with the bullets we found in the magazine."

"Any prints on the gun?"

"One small set. A woman's."

Branden wasn't surprised and let it show.

"Mike, I want to know where you got that pistol," Robertson said forcefully.

"I'll tell you, if it can be linked to a murder."

"Is this Hawkins's gun?"

"Sharp razor, Bruce. Sharp razor. Do you really think Hawkins would be the kind of guy to leave his murder weapon lying around for someone to find?"

Robertson stared at Branden for a long time and said flatly, "You're making yourself an accomplice, Mike."

Frowning, Branden shook his head, and said, "I need to talk with Marty Holcombe."

He left Robertson standing in front of the jail, headed north on Clay Street, and came immediately to the intersection with Route 62, called Jackson Street in its stretch through town. The tan and salmon-colored sandstone courthouse sits on the southeast corner of that intersection, sharing the block with the monument lawn and the jail. Branden waited for the light to change and idly studied the small downtown area.

The copper-green roof of the courthouse stood out distinctly against a blue sky that held a few clouds of cotton white. There were several workers tending to flowers at the base of the Civil War monument. Five Amish children stood beside mom and dad, who were seated on one of the old cast-iron benches along the sidewalk. The traffic on the streets was routine, mostly cars and trucks, some buggies, and an occasional tour bus.

He crossed Jackson with the light and covered the two blocks north to Perkins. Left on Perkins took him to the *Holmes Gazette* building, where Marty Holcombe was expecting him in his office looking out onto the street from a first-floor window. They went over what each of them knew about the Bromfield-Hawkins-Sands affairs, and Holcombe let Branden read the early stories that Bromfield had prepared.

Branden finished them and asked, "That's all there is? Cal

Troyer knew all of this about Hawkins long ago. So, probably, did most of the people in his church."

"Knew that Hawkins served in Vietnam?" Holcombe asked, somewhat puzzled. "Special Forces? CIA?"

"They've known everything about David Hawkins that you know and probably more. So has the family of his Amish fiancée."

"Paints a fairly raw picture," Holcombe argued.

"Not raw enough to warrant murder," Branden said.

Holcombe took back the typed pages, stacked them on edge, dropped them into a file drawer in his desk, and closed the drawer. He drummed his thumbs on his desk and thought. When he leaned back in his chair, the editor said, "Bromfield was just a kid, Mike. I hired him fresh out of Ohio University with a degree in journalism. A young kid with a girlfriend and a quiet future at a newspaper in a sleepy country town."

Branden listened.

"He wanted to do the Janet Hawkins murder story because it was so unusual. I figure he followed things up and got killed before he could bring the last of his story in to me."

Branden asked, "Do you have all of his notes before that?"

"Yes," Holcombe answered. "And I know most of the early leads he traced down."

"Did he talk to Sands?"

"First thing. Didn't learn much, though. It did give him the idea of looking into the prison records in New Jersey. Robertson had checked there before him, but I guess Bromfield got something new, being there in person."

"Did Bromfield talk to anyone else for the story?"

"He tried to talk to David Hawkins himself, but he was never home. Never did find him."

"That's all you've got, Marty?"

"There was the retired security guard. Some funny-name Greyson."

"Nabal Greyson."

"Right, Nabal. What kind of name is that?"

Branden shrugged. "Cal Troyer says it's Old Testament. Do you know anything about Greyson?"

"There's very little about him in any of Bromfield's notes, but Greyson seemed inconsequential to us. Lucky break to have been there when Sands was captured. He's told Robertson that he was here to see the Amish—you know, a tourist, but he took an apartment downtown when Robertson asked him to stay for the trial. The mayor intends to give him some kind of ceremony next week before Sands goes to court. But beyond that, I think Bromfield pretty much wrote him off."

Branden sat in his chair, eyes focused on the carpet, and then asked, "Anything else?"

Holcombe studied the professor's face for a moment as if he were mulling over a puzzle. "Mike, you said Bruce Robertson figures this is going to be a straightforward act of revenge? Hawkins on Sands I mean."

"Robertson does," Branden answered. "I don't."

"Then I've got a problem," Holcombe said. "I want to run Eric Bromfield's stories. Can't do that, though. Not just yet."

Branden asked, "Because of Robertson?"

"Partly," Holcombe said. "Robertson has asked me to hold off a spell. But there's another reason."

Holcombe lifted the receiver on his phone, punched in the audex code, listened to a recent message, skipped backward through the rest, found the one he wanted, and handed the receiver to Branden. Holcombe punched again on the phone and Branden heard Bromfield's voice.

"Marty, this is Eric. I'm in New Jersey. The state prison in Trenton. I can't run it all down for you now, but there's more here than just Jesse Sands. Hold those stories. I'm flying home tonight."

11

Tuesday, June 10
10:30 A.M.

BEFORE leaving the newspaper offices, the professor read through the few notes in Bromfield's desk on the Janet Hawkins murder. They revealed nothing about the trip to New Jersey, and nothing much about David Hawkins, either, considering how open Hawkins had been with Cal Troyer about his past. The only information Branden found helpful was a downtown address for Nabal Greyson.

The address was in an alleyway off Jackson Street, where Branden found a door to a narrow flight of stairs. It was in one of the old city buildings so often photographed by tourists on the square. The tall, ornate windows on the upper floors were set deeply into gray stone, with the brick trim painted black. The shutters were painted a soft rose. The steep, cramped staircase was a relic from another era. It had been remodeled and was now well lighted. The walls had been painted a light chocolate brown, and the iron steps had shiny black rubber treads.

He took the stairs past a first-floor music store and a second-floor law office and came to the third floor, which served as a residential hotel. A sign on the stairwell door indicated that rooms were available by the week or the month.

On the third-floor landing, Branden stopped to rest at a window looking out upon the square. He saw five or six young

Amish fellows joking together at the light. An assortment of semi tractor trailer rigs making the turn to follow 62 south out of town. One buggy at the hitching rail behind the old courthouse.

In a narrow hallway of the old building, he found Greyson's door number and knocked. In the apartment across the hall, he heard a shuffle, and out of the corner of his eye, Branden saw the door open a slight crack and then close. As Greyson answered his door, a metal security chain drew tight on the inside and stopped the door after it had opened an inch. A soft, raspy voice spoke from behind the chain.

"Yes?"

"Mr. Greyson?"

"Yes," he said again, with a hoarse, painful sound. Through the crack in the door Branden noted the pungent aroma of old cigars.

Branden began. "My name is Michael Branden," he said. "I'd like to talk with you about the Janet Hawkins murder."

"I've already given a complete statement to the police," Greyson said and coughed.

"I'm not with the police, Mr. Greyson. I'm trying to find David Hawkins as a favor to his fiancée's family."

"Do you know Hawkins?"

"No. I've simply been asked to help find him now that his daughter is dead. He seems to be missing."

"I doubt that I could help you any," Greyson said tentatively.

Branden noted a leading tone. Greyson lit the stub of a cigar from behind the door and seemed to invite conversation as he lingered in the smoke.

"Mr. Greyson, I understand that you captured Jesse Sands. I'd like to talk with you about that. Perhaps something you remember will help me find Hawkins."

Greyson slipped out of Branden's view and closed the door without speaking. Branden waited, not knowing whether to try again or go home to Caroline. After a pause sufficient to allow Greyson to think, the chain rattled slack, and the door opened.

Branden saw immediately that Nabal Greyson was a badly weathered man. He appeared disheveled and tired. His face betrayed a sense of weariness, and his dress was careless. The cigar in his teeth seemed to account for his irregular voice.

Greyson's one-room apartment revealed little about its temporary inhabitant. The furnishings were simple in the extreme. The bed was unmade. A sink and counter ran along the back wall, centered under a small window that admitted light past soiled yellow curtains. There were no personal effects in the room, apart from a police band radio that squawked periodically on the counter.

Greyson crossed the small room ahead of Branden and turned the volume on the scanner down to a faint mutter of squad cars, dispatchers, and ambulances. "I've been in the private security business twenty-two years," he explained in his crackling voice, "and I still haven't managed to retire completely. I listen to the public safety frequencies out of habit. Beats anything on radio or TV."

Greyson's attitude had turned noticeably more friendly, and he offered the professor a seat.

"I'm having a scotch," Greyson said as he turned to the sink. "Can I get you anything?"

"Nothing for me, thanks," Branden said, studying Greyson as he poured a fresh drink for himself at the counter. Greyson had pasty gray hair, combed back tightly against a pallid scalp. His nose was of a classic Roman style, hawk-like and prominent, his lips thin. His eyes were flat gray, their near-colorless quality accentuated by the moist-pink tone of his swollen eyelids. Above one eye, in a line glancing downward toward the bridge of his nose, there were four small, regularly spaced, scarlike depressions, as if he had once been stabbed there with a dinner fork.

Branden took a seat on a worn sofa and watched Greyson roll his dash of scotch slowly around in the bottom of a tall and narrow glass. Greyson pulled up a straight-backed kitchen chair and straddled it in front of Branden. Greyson studied the professor from his chair and took a swig of the scotch.

His first question to the professor was broad and general. "Why don't you tell me everything you can about the case, Mr. Branden."

"Actually, I don't know that much about it," Branden said. "I had hoped you could tell me more."

"Sorry. My part in the whole affair was rather brief. Heard the call on the scanner in my car and managed to grab the killer as he fled the house. If I were still a guard, it would have been 'in the line of duty' and nothing more. As it is, I just did what anybody else would have done. Nothing out of the ordinary."

The slender glass of scotch precessed from the tips of Greyson's fingers, and the ice clattered against the glass. Greyson fixed his eyes on the swirling whiskey and asked, "I assume you've been to the sheriff and the newspaper offices?"

"Just came from the paper, in fact, but Marty Holcombe didn't know much beyond . . ."

Greyson held up his hand to stop the professor. He turned to hear the police scanner more clearly, eventually deciding it was not a call that interested him. "Sorry," he said. "Thought I might have heard something. You were saying?"

"Do you listen to the scanner every day?" Branden asked.

"As I said, I've never quite gotten out of the habit. I feel more alive while I'm listening. Now, you had mentioned the newspapers. I don't recall having read much about myself in the papers."

"They didn't have much to go on, I take it," Branden said.

"I prefer it that way, Mr. Branden. I have no desire for publicity, and once this case is over, I'll quietly move on. I was in

Holmes County to see the sights, but now I'm just doing the sheriff a favor by sticking around until a court date some time next week or so."

As he rolled his drink, Greyson brought his cigar up to his lips and drew slowly on it. He looked at the professor slightly sideways around the cigar, eyes closed partway against the smoke, and asked a further question. "What can you tell me about Hawkins?"

"Not much, I'm afraid," Branden said, cautiously. "I'd like to find him, is all. And I've grown curious about him, although I've never met him."

"Why does he warrant your curiosity?" Greyson asked.

"The sheriff is concerned about revenge."

"Would you blame him? After all,"—Greyson stopped swirling his scotch and drained the glass—"it was his daughter."

"You said you were a security guard?" Branden asked, probing.

"I started out as an armed guard for one of the east coast casinos. But I eventually started my own company. I still own it, but I'm retired. I let the younger men walk the shifts, now, Professor."

"How did you know I'm a professor?" Branden asked.

"I have a lot of time on my hands, Dr. Branden, and I often take walks around town. The college is an excellent place for a retired gentleman to take an evening stroll. And who could miss the photographs of the college's most distinguished professor? Named a building after you, didn't they?"

"Just a wing of the library," Branden said.

"Don't be so modest, Dr. Branden. You're one of the nation's leading experts on period firearms, and there's that famous cannon of yours, fired each Fourth of July. People all over know about that. A *National Geographic* article, wasn't it? Look. I'm sorry I didn't let on that I knew who you were. But I was interested in what you had to say about Hawkins, and it just never became convenient to mention it to you. You understand, don't you?"

The scanner at the back of Greyson's little one-room apartment interrupted Branden's answer. Greyson turned to listen to the voice on the scanner and then walked over to the kitchen counter where it sat. When he had heard what he needed, Greyson pulled back the drab curtain on his little window, looked out, and motioned for Branden to come and have a look, too.

Below on the courthouse square, Cal Troyer was walking between two deputies to the front entrance of the red brick jail.

12

Tuesday, June 10
11:30 A.M.

THE *figure watching at the window realized there was no need
to follow Branden now, as he stepped out onto Jackson Street
and crossed to the jail. More to the point, to follow now might
be counterproductive. And the sheriff doesn't understand any
more than Branden does, he told himself. No point trying to
learn anything, now, from either of them. Just wait for the bugs
to do their job.*

*But the bugs had been a miserable failure. He had planted
two at the Brandens' and they hadn't picked up a thing. Nothing on the phone and nothing in the living room. That was
crazy. Surely they were talking, but where?*

*It'd be too risky to go back now to check the bugs, but he
knew he'd have to chance it, sooner or later. It was either that,
or go blind on the Brandens and what they knew.*

*Too many things to attend to, now. Should be preparing for
the day when Sands was brought out for trial.*

*Cal Troyer had started it all. So, he thought, I'll wire him up
too. More to worry about. But the whole point of doing this in
the first place was to get away with it. Get away with all of it. To
be caught would only be stupid. So play it safe, he told himself.*

*He moved away from the window and made his routine
weapons check. A light, rapid touch under his left arm and he
knew that the .45 was still in its place. Of all the people who*

might pose a threat, surely Branden posed the greatest. Back to the belt line, and there was the new Browning .22. The reporter had been too easy. A tap of the left ankle to the inside of the right ankle, and there was the little featherweight .38, somewhat under-powered, but better than a knife.

If the reporter had been easy, the professor would be downright troublesome. But still, what could Branden learn? The problem was, if Branden learned anything at all . . .

He remembered the reporter, and it settled him into a calmer mind. He relived the moment, standing in the narrow delivery alley between the newspaper offices and a downtown department store. Bromfield might have been suspicious, but not in time to have saved himself.

Stop obsessing, he admonished himself. Sit tight and do the job. One last job. They're not going to figure it out in time. It's too complicated for a country sheriff. Too involved for a small-time professor. They may get some of it, but by then it won't matter. They'll never see it coming. If they do, it'll simply be their funerals, too.

13

Tuesday, June 10
11:50 A.M.

"KNOCK it off, Bruce, this is crazy." Branden was planted solidly in the doorway to Robertson's office. His expression was angry, and his tone was uncharacteristically harsh.

Robertson sat coolly behind his desk, manifestly unconcerned about Branden's anger. Cal Troyer sat in a straight chair facing the sheriff's desk like a suspect. Deputies Wilsher and Schrauzer stood formally behind Troyer.

Cal idly turned the thin frames of his glasses on his fingertips, looking wearily down.

"It's OK, Mike," he said with resignation.

"It's not OK," Branden said and stepped farther into the office.

"You two can leave us," Robertson said, waving offhand at his deputies.

Branden made an obvious effort to keep his anger in check until the deputies had cleared the doorway. As soon as they were out of the office he started up again. "Bruce, if Cal tells you he doesn't know where Hawkins is, then he doesn't know. It's as simple as that, and you know it as well as anyone."

"I know nothing of the kind," Robertson said.

"That's not like you, Bruce. You know Cal as well as I do, and I'm telling you, if you don't back off now, you're gonna wreck more than one friendship here."

Robertson pressed ahead. "Cal, if I find out you're hiding . . . "

Branden took a step forward, but Cal cut him off, saying calmly, "Bruce, I'm not going to tell you this again. I don't know where Hawkins is."

"Then help me with the bishops out there. They're not saying a word."

Cal said, "I'd be disappointed if they did. Hawkins has been baptized, and they'll protect him."

The sheriff waved a dismissive hand in the air and looked for an instant as if he'd have more to say.

Branden said, "David Hawkins wouldn't have murdered Bromfield just for printing his life story."

"I'll wait for Phil Schrauzer to tell me that," Robertson snapped.

"What's that supposed to mean?" Branden said.

"He's leading up my investigation of the Bromfield murder. Interviewing friends, neighbors. Retracing his steps just before he died."

"Now that's more like it," Cal said.

"I want Hawkins," Robertson insisted.

Cal shook his head.

To Branden, Robertson said, "Where'd you get that pistol?"

"Have you got any evidence connecting it to the Bromfield murder?"

"OK, look, you two. Even if Hawkins didn't kill Bromfield he might still very well make an attempt on Jesse Sands."

"You've got nothing to suggest that," Branden said.

"He's disappeared," Robertson said.

"Doesn't mean anything," Branden said coolly.

"He tried to kill Sands that night at the jail."

"But he didn't," Cal said.

"I've got the note he taped to Sands's window."

"Can you prove that David did that?" Cal challenged.

"Who else?" Robertson shot back.

Branden said, "Bruce, you're going to find that Bromfield and Sands are alike in one respect. Neither of them has anything to do with Hawkins.

Robertson snorted.

"All right, then," Branden said impatiently. "All you have to do is guard Sands through his trial. Don't give Hawkins a chance at him."

"I don't intend to," Robertson scoffed. "We'll get Sands to trial, and then we can let the Bromfield case sort itself out. Either way, I still want to question Hawkins."

"You're gonna take this too far," Cal muttered.

"You don't have to take the weight like this, Cal," Robertson said.

"I've said everything I intend to," Cal said, eyes leveled at the sheriff.

"You'd better talk him down, Cal. You know as well as anyone that if Hawkins has intentions to murder Sands, there isn't much anyone could do to stop him."

Cal said nothing.

Robertson glowered at the pastor silently.

Branden wondered what there'd be left of the friendship if Robertson kept it up.

Robertson closed his desk drawer and said gruffly, "OK, Cal. You're calling the play. Just don't forget I warned you." He slowly pushed his large frame up from behind his desk and joined his two deputies out in the hall, closing the door as he left.

Inside, Branden and Troyer drew their chairs close to one another and whispered. Branden told Cal the places he intended to inquire about Hawkins, and Cal urged Branden to get out to the Raber farm. Branden told Cal what Robertson had done with the gun Abigail had produced. As if in response, Cal reached into his back jeans pocket, pulled out a single key, and gave it circumspectly to the professor. As the sheriff ambled back into the office, Cal whispered to Branden, "Hawkins's back basement."

14

Tuesday, June 10
2:15 P.M.

CAROLINE and Michael Branden found the Hawkins residence on its narrow west-end street overlooking the wide Killbuck valley. There, the marshes stretch out toward the distant hills in a flat, misty patchwork of wetlands, running for nearly thirty miles in a swatch that starts near Wooster to the north and falls down through Wayne and Holmes Counties as far south as the little village of Killbuck itself. In the west end of Millersburg, the old houses are set close together, sometimes little more than a driveway separating one from another.

A jumble of cars was parked along the street, some of them haphazardly pulled up onto muddy tree lawns. There were a few curbs still in place, and most had either a truck or a sedan parked beside them, sometimes with the wheels angled up onto the concrete. Only a few of the cars were late models. The rest were in varying states of repair. In front of one old house there was a restored army jeep, World War II vintage, freshly painted in camo colors of muted browns and forest greens.

Most of the houses in the neighborhood had old front porches, some open, some screened, and some boxed in with storm windows. There were houses with white wood siding, and there were some with shingles in faded browns and yellows. One house was painted a vivid blue, with creamy white trim. Another was covered on the north side with pink insulation panels, and a stack of aluminum siding lay in disorder under a ladder. The Hawkins place was a nondescript white-sided, two-story prairie home with two attic dormers facing the street. Yellow crime scene police ribbon stretched across the front door.

Caroline cupped her hands around her eyes and peered in through a front-porch windowpane of dirty glass. Branden unlocked the front door, using the key that Cal had given him at the jail. They stepped from the front porch into the living room and noticed a musty, lifeless odor. The tattered living room furniture was old and plain. The flocked golden wallpaper was in a style that had been popular in the fifties. The wood trim had been painted white throughout, giving the impression of never-remodeled age.

Branden glanced briefly up the stairwell on the right, and they crossed from the living room into the dining room. In the dining room, there was an old and massive, ornate dining room table pushed to the side, and a scattering of glass in the corner by a broken china hutch. There was also a sizable brown patch of dried blood on the wooden floor and on the matted wool carpet under the table.

Caroline asked, "Get the impression David Hawkins hasn't spent five minutes in this house since the night his daughter was killed?"

In the kitchen, there were a few unwashed plates and two pans crusted over with a forgotten meal. The storm door on the back porch was latched, but the outside screen door was smashed outward and hung open at an angle on its broken hinges.

Branden turned back into the kitchen and said, "Cal said we should get to Hawkins's back basement. He said it that way. 'Back basement.' Like a room."

In the corner of the kitchen, beside the swinging door into the dining room, they found a second door that opened to a landing at the side of the house. The landing let out onto the driveway where their car was parked, and it also led to the stairs to the basement. Caroline threw the light switch at the top of the landing, and they descended the stairs. Downstairs, they found an extraordinary half-basement room.

There were a number of professional-grade machinist tools covered with fitted plastic dustjackets as well as several woodworking machines, spaced generously and evenly around the room. The Brandens separated and circled among the tools. There were the old-style green metal drill presses and lathes, all in immaculate condition. The professor pulled the lever on a drill press, and it arched smoothly downward, clean and oiled to perfection. The metal bench of the press shined bright like stainless steel. Caroline threw the switch on a lathe, and it whirled and spun almost noiselessly. In all of the room, there was not so much as a single metal shaving scrap to be found. The woodworking tools were in the same condition. A tabletop saw, swept clean of sawdust. A radial arm saw that pulled out effortlessly along its slotted glide path.

The floor was of poured concrete, painted battleship gray. Several small drain holes each accepted a small rubber hose. The hoses were piped to three dehumidifiers that hummed quietly from their perches on rubber dampers.

Caroline studied the ceiling and then moved to the drill press and looked up to a light above the press. The ceiling light was positioned in precisely the spot that would best illuminate the work at the press.

"The lights were planned for the tools," Caroline said.

"He knew what he was doing," Branden agreed.

The concrete block walls on three sides of the basement room were painted ceiling white. There was neither a single crack in the walls nor a patch of crumbling mortar. The basement windows were sealed with new red brick, and would admit no light. Neither would a basement light, however bright, shine to the outside.

The fourth wall started about where the top riser of the basement stairs hit the landing overhead. The wall was made of white plasterboard panels, with only the thinnest of seams showing between them.

"Cal said 'back basement,' I'm almost certain," Branden said.

Caroline climbed the steps, went out onto the driveway, took a circuit around the house, and came back down.

"There are five basement windows, Michael," she reported. "Two here and three more in back."

The professor started under the stairs and Caroline started against the far wall. She worked her way around the lathe and back toward him. He worked toward her, and found nothing on the first pass.

On a second pass under the stairs, Branden looked up to study the wall and the risers with a penlight and found a small square of wood that did not precisely match the oak of the risers. He leaned back under the steps, craned his neck to look up, and then pulled the wood block from its place. Inside the small rectangular cavity behind the block, there was a toggle switch. When he flipped the switch, they heard the whirring of small electric motors behind the wallboards.

Together they pushed with their fingertips on the right seam of the nearest panel. Then they tried on the left, and the panel opened inward on its hinges. The professor reached in on the left and found a light switch. He pushed the panel open and led Caroline into David Hawkins's private arsenal.

There were guns, knives, and battle rifles of every description. Handguns filled glass-topped cases, and rifles hung on the walls. There was a riot shotgun, with a large circular magazine hanging under the barrel, as well as several double-barreled sporting shotguns. The waist-high display cases against three walls held revolvers and semiautomatic pistols—everything from Smith and Wesson revolvers to the H&K squeeze-cocker

9 mm, with the characteristically wide grip that was contoured in front for the shooter's fingers. A matched pair of Ruger Government Target .22s, the Mark II variety with 6.5-inch barrels, lay in the case. Also an old .44 Auto Mag and an imposingly large .50-caliber, Israeli Desert Eagle. Shelves above the display cases held other handguns and gear. There were a dozen or so military long guns on a vertical rack in one corner. Several had bayonets and military slings made of brown leather or woven khaki. Branden lifted one of the longer rifles, a Fabrique Nationale FAL .308 with a British illuminated battle scope, and held it to his eye. When he lowered the rifle, he noticed a small white paper tag hanging from a string on the trigger guard. It read "sighted 300 yds, Federal Match Grade, 168 grain boat-tail hollow points." He made a quick visual check of the other long guns in the room and saw that they too, whether military or sporting, bore similar tags that specified range and style of cartridge.

Branden noted an early-version M16 with the first triangular forestock, and no forward assist. A thirty-round magazine was attached under the receiver, just forward of the pistol-style grip. He identified an Israeli Military Industries Uzi pistol—small, heavy, and fitted with a collapsible, metal shoulder stock. Several Russian AK-47s stood on a rack. There was one battered SKS rifle with a plain and inexpensive wooden stock, bayonet, and Chinese insignias on top of the iron sights. Two H&K Model 91 automatic rifles were mounted on a wall. Branden recognized them as probably the most expensive items in the lot, and they each had switches that would change the fire mechanism from semiautomatic to fully automatic. On the wall above the rifles, there was a fully automatic H&K MP5 machine pistol, with a long, thin, 9 mm magazine mounted in front of the trigger guard. A fully automatic MAC 11 machine pistol hung shoulder high on the wall next to the secret door. Beside the small machine gun, there were six long magazines attached to the wall. Branden took one down from its clip and found it loaded. He depressed the top round, noticed that it sank into the magazine only a fraction of an inch, and said, "Thirty rounds, fully loaded."

Against the fourth wall of the back armory room, there was a long workbench about waist high. Under the bench there were racks of small metal drawers, plus stacks of green army-surplus ammo cans. Each drawer and each can was marked with a different caliber. Caroline pulled one drawer open and lifted out a handful of copper coated projectiles.

Branden gave them a glance and said, "9 mm. Full metal jackets."

On top of the long bench, Hawkins had mounted several die presses. Branden pulled the arm down on one of them, and the ram for a .45 bullet die rose into position where a projectile would be seated into a brass case.

"Reloading presses," Branden said. "Hawkins makes his own cartridges."

Caroline pulled a bound notebook from one of the shelves over the workbench and leafed through it. She chose an entry at random and read it aloud for her husband.

> Lot Number 1523
> 220 SWIFT, 55 grain Hornady Boattail, FMJ
> Federal cases trimmed to 2.196 +/- 0.001"
> CCI Benchrest primers seated 0.002"
> 43.70 +/- 0.02 grains of IMR 4350 = 3800 fps
> c.o.l. = 2.680 +/- 0.001"

The professor came over and took down another notebook for himself.

He studied it for a minute or so and then said, "It's load data. The prescription for making up a cartridge. It specifies the case, primer, powder, projectile, and c.o.l."

"What's c.o.l.?"

"It stands for case overall length." He read another page and said, "These powder charges are specified to the nearest two one-hundredths of a grain. The c.o.l. to the nearest one-thousandth of an inch."

"That's significant?" Caroline asked.

"It's excessive," Branden said. "Most reloaders get it to the tenth of a grain and go with that. My grandfather used to scoop in powder until it looked right to him and almost never bothered even weighing a powder charge, much less weighing one to a hundredth of a grain."

The logbooks were arranged in chronological order. Branden took down the latest book, opened to the last entry and read:

> Lot 2155
> 6 mm PPC, 75 grain Hornady hollow points
> Remington cases trimmed to 1.505 +/- 0.001"
> CCI Benchrest primers, seated 0.002 inches
> 24.30 +/- 0.02 grains IMR 4198 = 3110 fps
> c.o.l. = 2.102 +/- 0.001 inches

It was dated three days ago.

"I think that's a target load," Branden said absently. He turned slowly in place, looking for the rifle that would match the cartridge, and failed to find it.

He walked over to the wall panel they had pushed open to enter the custom room. He swung it closed, and on the back they saw the weapon that matched the target round from the last entry in Hawkins's load book.

The rifle that hung on the back of the door had a stainless steel barrel and a blue-sparkle polymer stock with extravagant features. The cheek plate was custom molded and unusually tall. The forestock was flattened and tapered. The thumbhole in the stock was cut for a personal fit to one man's hand. The barrel was fluted. The action was a custom remake of a standard Remington 700 bolt. There was an enormous 36-power Leupold scope mounted on top. The machined silver steel gave it a look of enormous power and precision.

Beside the rifle there was a framed photograph of a man holding the rifle and a trophy. The caption below the photo read:

> David Hawkins, Millersburg, Ohio
> Grand Champion
> 1989 Benchrest Internationals
> Erlanger's Range

Beneath the photo, there was a target mounted in another frame. It was hand lettered in the margins, with pencil.

Caroline bent over and read the lettering out loud. "Five rounds. 6 mm PPC. 200 yards."

The target contained a single bullet hole about six millimeters in diameter. The bullet hole had missed the small bull's-eye on the target. Instead, it sat curiously on the page, well away from the bull's-eye, a single six-millimeter hole, about an inch and a half high-right.

"Is it possible that only one bullet hit the target?" Caroline asked.

Branden shrugged and said, "Cal wanted us to see all of this."

"Why?"

"Don't know," Branden said. "Cal knows about this room. I'd be willing to bet there aren't two other people in Millersburg who do."

"Plus us makes five," Caroline added.

"Cal is standing by Hawkins."

"Then why tell us about these guns?"

"To convince us he's right."

Caroline gave a little nervous laugh that clearly said Cal had not succeeded with her.

Branden studied the target on the back of the secret door. He held the rifle a moment longer and then lifted it to his eye. The butt of the stock hit him at the round of his shoulder, but when he laid his face softly against the tall cheek plate, the eyepiece of the scope hit him above the eyebrow. "Long neck," he said to himself.

"Long neck?" Caroline asked.

"The stock's custom built for one man alone. The scope is high for me. Hawkins has got himself a long neck."

Branden hung the rifle behind the door and said, "I've seen enough."

After Caroline had left the room, he hit the lights, stepped back through the secret door, and shut it from outside in the machine shop. He worked the hidden switch to throw the electric bolts home, replaced the block of wood that hid the switch, and climbed the steps behind Caroline.

In their car in the driveway, Branden sat a moment with the motor running, absently tapping his thumbs against the steering wheel and thinking of what they had just seen in the custom basement room. As they sat there, Ricky Niell came slowly up to the driver's side in his immaculate black and gray deputy sheriff's uniform. Laying his right arm atop the roof of the car, he bent over to the window and rapped at the glass with the knuckles of his left hand. Branden jerked almost imperceptibly but recovered quickly and rolled the window down, wondering if Niell had watched them go into the house as well as come out. He switched the engine off.

"Recognized your car, Professor," the deputy said cheerfully.

"Ricky," Branden said. "I see Robertson has you on the clock."

Niell laughed and shrugged. "Something like that. More to the point, he has me on you."

Branden looked first to Caroline, who arched an eyebrow, and then to Niell, who was still leaning over at the professor's window.

"Look, Professor, I thought you might like to know that Robertson sent Cal Troyer home about ten minutes after you left."

Branden muttered, "More of his games."

"I don't think he's playing games," Niell said.

"He wants Hawkins, and all the rest is just games," Branden said.

"Cal Troyer is a way to Hawkins," Niell said.

"Cal said he can't help, and I believe him," Branden said. "He truthfully doesn't know where Hawkins is."

"I think Hawkins is only part of the problem," Niell said. He looked down, studied the blacktop beside the sedan, hesitating awkwardly as he considered what more he could safely tell the Brandens without running foul of the sheriff's specific orders. Eventually he added, "The sheriff is not going to ease off on Hawkins until Jesse Sands goes to state prison." He watched the professor's expression for a reaction.

Branden said, "If Cal says he can't help find Hawkins, then he can't do it, and that is the long and the short of it, Ricky. If Robertson pushes there, a long-time friendship is going to crumble away."

Niell looked to Caroline, held her eyes for a spell, and then said directly to the professor, "Then all I can tell you is that Cal Troyer is going to be on the hot seat until next week, because Robertson believes Troyer can deliver Hawkins."

"Why next week?" Branden asked.

"Next week, Friday, Jesse Sands is going to trial, and Robertson's got it figured that that's when we'll hear from David Hawkins."

Branden shook his head and frowned.

Caroline asked, "Ricky, do you know where Cal went after he left the jail?"

Niell said, "Troyer drew me aside and asked me to tell you two that he'd be pitching hay." Then he looked into the car, waiting for one of the Brandens to translate. Neither did.

As Niell headed back down the drive, the professor smiled, remembering the little map that Cal had drawn to the Raber farm.

15

Tuesday, June 10
6:00 P.M.

CAL Troyer was dressed about as close to Amish as he could
get, but still not quite be there. His old straw hat was the proper
straw hat, creamy yellow with a plain black band. His black
vest hung casually open, but it was assuredly the proper black
vest. The sleeves on his light blue shirt were rolled up to the
correct spot on his elbows. But a few crucial details were out of
sorts. His blue jeans were Levis, not the plain denim the Rabers
wore. He used a belt rather than cloth suspenders. And he wore
Reeboks instead of lace-up boots. Other than that, the only
thing that gave him away readily was his full, white beard, not
shaved smooth above and below the mouth.

He worked in the tall barn next to a wagonload of new-dried
hay. There was the sweet aroma of the new hay and a swarm
of insects. The horses whinnied in their harnesses and stomped
at the dirt floor. The odor of manure was strong. The barn was
cool, and the work was steady. Today, the Raber boys had
helped their father gather in his crop, and tomorrow, they'd all
help the oldest son on his south fields. All of the men were
there, and so were all of the boys, the lot of them dressed alike.
The weather looked good for making hay—sunshine and gentle
breezes, with no change in sight.

Cal threw pitchforks of the loose hay from the flat wooden
wagon up to Joshua, the youngest Raber son. Joshua dispersed

it toward the back of the loft. Other brothers worked with the senior Raber to bale the remainder of the hay using a gasoline engine outside the barn. Cal had put in five hours in the fields, and it was understood that he would stay for supper.

When the last wagon had been emptied, Joshua unhitched the team from the wagon and, following behind them with a whip, drove them, still in harness, into the other barn. Cal walked outside and stretched the muscles in his back and neck while he watched for Abigail at the big house.

The Raber barns were set low on a hillside, near a small stream. The Rabers' white frame house, two and a half stories, stood fifty yards farther up the hill. The tall windows were draped with aqua-green curtains that hung full length and straight inside. At the back of the house, there was a breezeway-style porch, with screened windows and a long oak-slatted porch swing suspended on springs from hooks in the ceiling. The breezeway led from the rear of the big house to a smaller, grand-parent's house in the back. It was in this small Daadihaus that Herman P. Raber now lived with his wife and their unmarried daughter Abigail. The oldest son, Herman H. Raber, lived with his family of fourteen in the big house.

The two red barns towered to three full stories, counting the lowest level, where the doors opened into a small ravine with a trickle of a summer stream. The stream bed was trampled by the hooves of dairy cattle and draft horses. There was fifty years of mud splattered against the foundation stones of the barn.

The two top levels of the biggest barn faced toward the house, away from the stream. There were cutouts in the high walls for swallows. A tall pole on a nearby mound held a two-level martin house. Along toward dusk, the martins and swallows came out and began their ballet overhead, scooping bugs from the air in swift, erratic, darting maneuvers, and steady, graceful, arching glides.

When the day's hay was in the barns, Cal joined the brothers at the brick well behind the house, and they pumped sulfur water for each other, to wash for supper. The cleaner, sweeter water in the attic tanks inside the big house was pumped up from a deeper formation by a windmill set on a rise behind the house.

At dinner, father Raber offered grace, giving thanks for the blessings of crops, family, and peace. The meal itself was substantial. Beef with heavy gravy. Mashed potatoes, and sweet potatoes with brown sugar. Beans, corn, and homemade breads. Reheated ham for those who wanted it. An assortment of fresh pies, all served on a long kitchen table with simple benches on its four sides. By the time the meal was finished and the women had begun collecting the dishes, the sun had set behind the windmill. After the meal, Cal and Raber Sr. sat together on the back porch swing as the other Rabers headed for their various chores.

Herman P. Raber was an extraordinarily short man, no more than five feet tall. His gray beard was tangled and heavy on his chin. His long, straight hair was thinning and had taken a set under the rim of his hat. His forehead above the hat line was creamy white. Below the hat line, it was tanned a deep red brown. His short fingers were callused and worn. There were large cracks in the skin, and these cracks held the dark stains of a lifetime spent close to the soil. His fingernails were broken and uneven, and the two smallest fingers on his left hand were missing, victims of a forgetful childhood moment when he had caught them in a reaper. His beard was stained yellow in the corner of his mouth where his pipe always had hung, and his index finger was brown from tamping the pipe. He wore small, round spectacles low down on his nose. His belly stuck out beneath his unbuttoned vest. He had a copper wrist band for arthritis and an iron band on one ankle. He wore no wedding ring. His boots, tonight, were unlaced because his feet were swollen from diabetes. He was fifty-seven years old, and he had known Cal Troyer for thirty years.

Cal spoke quietly in Low German dialect, expressing assurances that David Hawkins, whatever he was up to, would come home to the Raber farm. "He's made a commitment to Amish life," Cal said. "You know his resolve as well as any, Herman."

Raber puffed on his pipe and followed the lazy plumes of smoke with his eyes. After a while, he said, "I've got a cabin back over the hill. It was the original homestead that my great-grandfather built when he started out. Several generations have farmed the same land after him. Tilled the soil in their own days. Great-grandfather. Grandfather. My father, and now me. Not to mention the original lands divided to the sons and handed down faithfully through the generations.

"We live the same life today, on the same land as my great-grandfather. We keep the old ways because that is important to do. Certainly no one else is going to do that. Keep the old ways.

"And Hawkins can have his place among us. He and Abigail are to have the homestead cabin and fifty acres to get them started. But now I wonder. Don't think you can blame me either, with him disappearing the day Abi found his gun."

"You can't be certain that was his pistol," Cal said.

Raber shrugged and relit his pipe. "Who knows if an Englisher can truly honor the old ways?"

"What will it hurt to trust him, now?"

"It will hurt Abigail if our trust is misplaced."

Cal nodded. "Yes, but what of his vows?"

"I saw him take the vows, it's true," Raber said. "But you're asking me to buy a sack full of kittens, without looking into the sack."

Cal seemed uncertain.

Raber explained. "I'm going to look in the sack, Pastor. Wait to be sure about David Hawkins."

As they sat together and talked softly on the porch swing, the crickets came out and bordered them around in a blanket of peaceful sounds. There was the muffled stamping of horse's hooves on straw, their whinnies in the barn, and the low voices of the cows in the nearest fields. The tensions of city life drifted out of Cal Troyer, and he stopped trying to wrestle with the puzzle of David Hawkins. Then, toward nine o'clock, Mike Branden came hiking over the hill where the windmill stood.

The professor wore blue jeans, a light green Millersburg College jacket, and a flat-brimmed, Amish-black hat. Over his hiking boots, ankles, and shins, he had strapped yellow and blue nylon hiking gaiters. He paused to slip them off before coming around the porch to Cal and Raber Sr.

"Mr. Raber," Branden said. "My name is Mike Branden. I would be hoping to talk with you, and the pastor here, about David Hawkins."

Cal remained silent and, somewhat taken by surprise, curiously watched Branden pull briars off his jeans where the gaiters had failed to protect him.

Branden explained, "I hiked in across the bottoms about a mile and a half. Had to park over on County Road 229 in order to lose what I think was Bruce Robertson's tail."

"You thought they'd follow you here?"

"Ricky Niell was kind enough to tip me off," Branden said and looked to Mr. Raber and back to Cal.

Cal apologized and said, "Herman Raber, I'd like to present Professor Michael Branden. He's the one who spoke to Abigail."

Raber gave a little nod and lit his pipe without comment. Branden came onto the screened porch and pulled up a short, unpainted wooden chair beside the swing.

Cal said to Branden, "Mike, Hawkins is set up here about as nicely as a person could want. Mr. Raber has given Abigail the original farmstead and fifty acres for the day when they're to be married. David's got everything he's wanted, and I'll not readily believe he'll trade it all in for nothing."

"Cal, I saw what he's got stored away in his back basement room," Branden said and pointedly eyed his friend.

"And you saw that everything was there, in its place," Cal asserted. "Hawkins hasn't touched the stuff in months."

"I also saw that he's made a recent entry in his logbook. Only three day ago," Branden countered.

Cal swallowed hard and tried to cover his surprise. Mr. Raber eased forward on the swing and seemed interested.

"It doesn't mean anything," Cal said.

"Do you know he's a long-range marksman?"

"It doesn't mean a thing," Cal said again, sounding exasperated.

"Do you know that he can drill the heart out of a walnut at 200 yards?" Branden asked and glanced at Raber to see what reaction that would produce.

"That's only a hobby," Cal said.

The senior Raber said, "Hobbies don't put food on the table. Hunting does, so we hunt. But, killing people est verboten." Then he knocked out his pipe as if there were nothing more to be said on the subject, and retired to the little Daadihaus, leaving Branden and Troyer alone on the breezeway porch.

"Hawkins is not just another Vietnam veteran," Branden said. "He was U.S. Army Special Forces. CIA."

"Ex-Special Forces," Cal interrupted. "Ex-CIA."

"Whatever. But, he's that and also a long-range sharpshooter with a secret basement armory."

"I know all of this, Mike."

"He's a gun nut, Cal!"

"He likes to punch holes in paper targets."

"You're not worried even a little bit?"

"Not a fraction."

Branden realized that Cal would not soon change his mind about David Hawkins, so he stood and motioned for Cal to follow him to Cal's truck. "It's about time we got home, Cal," he said.

The little country road that borders the Raber farm cuts due south toward Mt. Hope. It rises and falls over steep hills and into secluded valleys, but never turns to the right or to the left in more than a dozen miles. On a peaceful summer day, it will see an abundance of buggy traffic and a few cars. At night, the buggies are mostly parked in their barns, and cars have few reasons to be going anywhere on such a back-country road.

Tonight, Cal drove Branden to his car on a deserted stretch of County Road 229. He pushed his pickup along through the dark, with his window down and the breeze toying with his beard. He drove in silence with his thoughts, and tried to solve the puzzle of what David Hawkins might do with new bullets.

When they reached the professor's truck, Cal pulled his old Chevy in behind it, and Branden sat pensively on the bench seat next to Cal. Off in the distance, there was the faint orange glow of a kerosene lantern through the sliding doors of an old barn. On ahead, the lights of a rare car stopped at a darkened intersection of county roads and then slipped away to the south. Cal turned the engine off, and soon the crickets started their cadence again.

"I need your help, Cal," Branden said, staring grimly at the windshield in front of him. "Even if you're right about Hawkins, we still need to find him before Robertson does. If nothing else, just to convince him to turn himself in."

"I doubt he'll do that, Mike."

"The Rabers and Abigail haven't seen him?"

"No."

"Robertson still wanted him when he questioned you at the jail?"

"Yes."

"Marty Holcombe thinks Hawkins could very well have killed Eric Bromfield to stop him from printing whatever it was that he learned in New Jersey."

Cal groaned feebly and laid his head against the back of the seat.

Branden turned his thoughts to Greyson and said, "Nabal Greyson has been hanging around since he captured Jesse Sands."

"That Old Testament name," Cal mused, his thoughts somewhere distant. "It's unusual." With his head back, his eyes were fixed in the dark on the ceiling in the cab of his truck.

"The man himself is unusual," Branden said. "Rather a messy old fellow with a taste for cigars."

"I think it's First Chronicles," Cal said, eyes still looking up. "Maybe First Samuel. Nabal, I mean. Strange name."

"He said Jesse Sands is to go to trial next week, and then he'll be moving on."

"So we've got until Friday to find David," Cal said.

"Robertson wouldn't argue with you there," Branden said. "So, where do we start?"

"Greyson might help."

"I got the impression he pretty much wants to stay out of it," Branden said.

"Try Holcombe again?" Cal suggested. He sat up and gripped the wheel.

"Holcombe said Bromfield had a girlfriend."

"She might be helpful."

"Right. I'll talk to her," Branden said

"Bromfield told Holcombe he had found something in New Jersey," Cal said.

"Right."

"What was that?"

"Don't know," Branden said.

"Does Holcombe know?"

"I don't think so."

"Then we've got to get to New Jersey," Cal said.

"I'll do that," Branden offered. "Seems like Jesse Sands is the key. Do you know what he said to David Hawkins that night at the jail?"

"No."

"It had to have been something so provocative that Hawkins has decided to kill Sands."

"If David were going to kill Jesse Sands, he'd have done it that night at the jail," Cal said. "You know he had Ricky Niell's gun."

The point hit home with Branden. Then he remembered the cardboard window note. "Cal, do you know the phrase 'It's mine to avenge. I will repay'?"

"Sure. It's New Testament verse. Romans. Also Hebrews. The whole thing goes: 'It is mine to avenge; I will repay. And again, The Lord will judge his people. It is a dreadful thing to fall into the hands of the living God.'"

Branden shook his head and muttered beneath his breath.

Cal said, "Hawkins knows that verse, and he knows what it means, Mike."

"Which is?" Branden asked.

"Plain enough, wouldn't you say? Vengeance is forbidden to men. God himself will avenge. Besides, God is better at it."

"Bruce'll just say Hawkins has got himself a 'God Complex' or something," Branden said.

"The verse is tied up with this?" Cal asked.

"Part of those verses was taped to Jesse Sands's jailhouse window. Big block letters, facing inward to the cell. It said, 'It is mine to avenge. I will repay.'"

"I can't believe it," Cal said, disturbed.

"What is it that you can't believe, Cal, the sign or Robertson's interpretation of it?" Branden asked.

"Both!" Cal fell silent, drew inward, and tapped nervously

at the wheel with his thumbs. His mind filled with the memories of David Hawkins's first year in Millersburg. Hawkins had sought out Cal at his little independent church. They had become close friends over the years. And Hawkins had told him the story of the time he had first seen Cal in Vietnam. But Hawkins had changed for the better, and had worked himself steadily away from his addiction to violence, toward a life of peacefulness. Cal remembered the months he and Hawkins had invested, chiseling away at the residue of his guilt and shame from the Vietnam war. Of the struggle to piece his life together after a lifetime of cold-hearted, soul-numbing missions. After a lifetime in the company of killers. His infatuation with guns, and death. His quickness to judge and to blame. The anger and excuses he had nurtured within himself. The heavy weight of dreadful memories that had driven him to Millersburg. The burdens of the heart that had brought him to Cal Troyer in the first place. And the bond that had been woven between them in the long hours of prayer that they had shared.

But then something had snapped inside of David Hawkins. Or so it now seemed. At least Robertson would say it had. But that, Cal told himself now, was impossible. It was impossible to believe that after finding his way at last, David Hawkins would throw his life away for this. For revenge. For anything at all, now that he had found Abigail.

Yet Cal Troyer also understood, as he sat in the truck with Branden, that whatever else might still develop between David Hawkins and Jesse Sands, whatever might have broken David Hawkins that night at the jail, whether Hawkins could understand it now or not, he and Branden were the two best hopes David Hawkins had of coming out of this whole. Of walking away unharmed from Jesse Sands. From the tragic murder of his daughter. And Cal understood, at the core of his soul and heart, that he owed David Hawkins the testimony of a better way. The chance to live his life guiltless of another man's blood.

Free of the same burdens that, before, had nearly destroyed him. To walk free into his new Amish life, without the price of Jesse Sands's murder on his head.

After a long, thoughtful pause, Cal said, "Mike, David Hawkins wasn't just Special Forces. He wasn't even just CIA."

Branden turned on his seat to face Cal.

Cal said, "In Vietnam and after, before he came to me, David Hawkins was the principal trigger on an elite two-man Special Forces team."

"He was a sniper, wasn't he, Cal."

"One of the best the army has ever trained."

"I guessed as much, when I saw his arsenal."

16

Tuesday, June 10
9:00 P.M.

WHEN Abigail Raber retired to her small bedroom on the first floor of the little Daadihaus, there was a note under her feather pillows. She held it up to the kerosene lantern on the nightstand and read its short message. With tears streaming down her cheeks, and with a consuming gratitude for an answered prayer, she gathered a shawl around her nightgown and sat down in great-grandmother's rocker to wait.

The small bedroom was furnished with only the sparest of essentials. There were no pictures on the wall and no mirror over the dresser. The deep purple curtains were entirely plain, and they hung in long, straight pleats to the floor. The floor was made of wooden boards, painted flat gray. The bed was puffy with down but somewhat lumpy from wear. It was covered with an ornate, handmade quilt. There was a washbowl and a large ceramic water pitcher on the nightstand. Her clothes hung on a plain iron bar against one wall, and her shoes were turned upside down on a rack with pegs near the door. She sat in the worn rocker with her eyes closed, but did not sleep.

The floor all around her feet was scattered with handmade baskets and the reeds from which she wove them. A sign out near the front road told passersby that the Rabers had baskets for sale, and over the years, she had made a great deal of money selling the baskets that had kept her busy on lonely nights, when she could only have dreamed of marriage. Before the summer when she had first met David Hawkins at the well.

At 2:30 A.M. she dressed, laced her high leather shoes, and eased quietly through the door of her bedroom. She moved carefully along the hall and out the front door near the breezeway porch. With a quarter moon low on the horizon, she made for the windmill and then dropped along a path through the bottoms where she had played as a child. Her feet found the path unerringly at night, relying on her memories. Her grandparents had lived in the cabin when she was a child, and the numberless trips she had made to that cabin gave her the way now in the dark.

The cabin stood at the edge of the woods along the easternmost Raber field. The path came over a rise, ran along the north edge of the field, dropped into the bottoms, and then skirted the woods for thirty yards. On the front porch she found the wagon her grandfather had made for her, years ago. The porch swing, where she had sat so many evenings with her grandmother, was down on the porch boards, the ropes having given out long ago. The old front door seemed as familiar to her as her very thoughts. The smells inside brought her an overwhelming, bittersweet assurance of connectedness and safety.

As her eyes sought him in the dark, he lit a match and then from it, a small candle in the corner, away from the window curtains. She crossed the room and held him passionately in her arms. They kissed by the light of the candle, and whispered "I love you" through their tears, Abigail awash in joy to be holding him again, David torn anew by her beauty and her love.

She lifted her head from his shoulder, and her eyes begged him for an answer. "David, where have you been?"

He gently pressed her head to rest again on his shoulder and whispered into her ear, "I have much to do, now, Abigail. Be patient."

"They say you're going to kill that man."

He held her away, peered deeply into her eyes, and said, "Trust me now, Abigail. It will be all right, I promise you."

"I have trusted you with my love, David. With our future. With my life. But they've all been looking for you."

"I know they have, Abigail. Don't worry. They'll never understand. The sheriff hasn't figured out everything, yet. When I am ready, he'll understand it all, but not until then. When the time comes, they'll all understand well enough."

"You are scaring me, David."

"You must trust me," he said, and then, "Tell me about the professor."

"He wants to help us."

"What's he like?"

"He is gentle. He looked at me with gentle eyes."

"He's the only one I worry about," Hawkins said. "He, if anyone, might stop me."

"I pray that he will," she whispered in new tears.

"Abigail, listen to me. I promise you this will not turn out wrong. You don't understand this any more than the rest of them do."

"I understand only that if you kill that man, my family will never accept you."

"I know that well enough, my love."

"Then what are you doing, David? Why have you disappeared from us?"

Hawkins sighed wearily and sank into a chair beside the small candle. His blond Amish-cut hair and whiskers were full grown. His clothes were perfectly, properly, altogether plain.

"David," she said, standing in front of his chair. "If you kill him, for the rest of your life you will carry the staggering burden of needless bloodshed. It'll wear you down, crush the life out of you. You'll be judged by God. You'll be blamed by men."

"You don't understand."

"What will become of us? Of our lives together? Please don't let me live out my days blaming you for the death of us."

"I know who to blame, Abigail," Hawkins said in a tone edged with bitterness.

"I know only that Father will blame you, and that we will never marry," Abigail whispered.

"You wouldn't leave your family for me?" he asked knowing the answer.

She gave no response other than the quiet tears that spilled from her eyes.

As he sat there, he drew her close to him and held her around her waist, his head pressed against her. Then he gently pulled her down to the chair beside him, and began to explain.

"Listen, Abigail. Please," he said and reached with a delicate hand to turn her eyes into his. "I will not come back until this is all finished."

She began to protest, but he held a finger lightly against her lips.

"Abigail," he said, in a gentle voice. "If I were to blame anyone for Janet's murder, who would it be?"

She looked back into his eyes with a blank expression, confused by the question.

"You would think Sands. Right?" Hawkins said. "But, how about the police? After all, they answered the call too late to save her. So why not blame them?"

He went on. "How about the 911 operator? She took too long on the phone."

He continued. "Why shouldn't I blame Nabal Greyson? He didn't swing that bat soon enough.

"How about Sheriff Robertson? He's not done anything other than look for me.

"How about the English who sell electric phones and then let citizens believe that 911 can save them from an intruder?

"Why don't I blame the fools in New Jersey who set Jesse Sands free?

"Abigail, trust me. If I were to kill all of those who are to blame for Janet's murder, I'd have to kill at least twenty people here and in New Jersey."

In the light of the candle, he saw a puzzled look on Abigail's face, a look curiously mingling fear, confusion, disquiet, and hope. Fear that David Hawkins could really blame them all. Confusion at the depth of his emotions. Disquiet knowing the desperate life from which he had fled. Hope, maybe blind faith, that he would do the right thing, now that he had found a new life with her.

"Abigail, can't you see? The very reason I love you is why I must do this now. The very reasons that I have sought the plain life among your brothers is why I have to finish this now, before I can have a life of peace with you. The very things that drove me from the world, the things that make the English ways so detestable to me now, are the things that force me to finish my life there, on my own terms, before I can come to you. I'll not have a life with you if I walk away from this now. You must believe me when I tell you that what I am about to do is the last thing that must be done before I can walk among the peaceful ones with truth and peace. This one thing that is left undone will take another week. Abigail, hang on to your hope until then. Wait only another week, and I will come to you."

As she walked back to the big house, the last cherishing words he had spoken to her were buried deep within her heart, where all her hopes for their future together were stored, now, in absolute trust. David Hawkins had promised her a future, and she clung to that. He had offered his life's promise to her on irrevocable terms, and she embraced that promise tonight with an unquenchable faith. She had taken the measure of the one man who had given her the gift of love, and her trust in him now brought her peace. With her mind clear and her heart tranquil,

Abigail remembered the last things he had said to her tonight, in the cabin where they soon would be married.

"Most of all, Abigail," he had said. "Know this above all else. No matter what you hear and no matter what they say, by the finish of next week, I will come home to you, on terms your father can accept. Abigail, I will come to you, and we will marry. I know what I am doing. Trust me now, my love, to do this one last English thing."

17

Wednesday, June 11
9:15 A.M.

"OH, listen, darlin'," one woman said to the other as they stood in front of Abigail's little roadside stand. "They gather the reeds themselves, off the land. It's the way they do everything, isn't that right, dear? Off the land."

Their husbands sat in the long Cadillac, dozing after an early lunch at the Harvestfest Authentic Amish Restaurant on Route 250 south of Kidron. The lady friend stood over Abigail's folding table and peeled off bills to pay for five baskets.

"Well, I know they make everything at home. That much I do know," the first chirped confidently. "I've been coming down here for four years now. But, do you, my dear?" she asked Abigail. "You know. Gather your own reeds off the land?" Both ladies waited eagerly for an answer.

Abigail had been selling baskets there beside the road for ten years. In those years, she had learned to listen to the prattlings of the English tourists without an opinion or a thought showing on her face. And she knew that a little broken English would help sales more than anything.

Abigail counted back change and said a few words in Low German. Then, haltingly, she said, "We gather, yes."

In an audible whisper, the veteran of four day-trips to Holmes County explained to her neophyte friend, "They don't speak that much English."

Abigail looked up and, in Low German, said the equivalent of, "We gather the reeds by post. They come in crates from an art supply wholesaler out of New York City."

The ladies smiled at the German, understanding nothing whatsoever of it, and then gathered up their baskets, roused their husbands, and drove off with the satisfying knowledge that they had garnered another secret of the mysterious Amish ways. Certain that they had unearthed another of the authentic mysteries of Holmes County, Ohio. Satisfied to have hunted down the kind of rare, personal experience that would carry the day at bridge games and lawn parties for weeks to come.

Abigail folded the bills, pushed them into a small cloth drawstring purse, dropped the purse into a brown grocery bag under her little table, and counted the baskets that remained. Only five hadn't sold, and now it seemed that there might not be enough. She had started the day with twenty-six.

Earlier, when she had returned to the Daadihaus after her visit to the cabin, Abigail had sat in her rocker until dawn, filled with a peacefulness she had rarely known before. By the light of her kerosene lamp, she had hummed the young people's songs, favorites at the Sunday socials, and she had changed the prices on all of her baskets. The first six or seven she had doubled, marking the new prices in pencil on each of the paper tags. Then, to be sure, she had changed them again, to triple her usual asking prices. Surely, she had thought, that would do it nicely. Triple the regular price on all of her baskets. It would take all day to sell even one. And today, Abigail had reasoned, she might very well need to sell by the road for a very long time. It all depended, now, on Cal Troyer.

With her baskets loaded into her small buggy, she had hitched her pacer at dawn. The buggy was light and fast, as everyone in those parts knew. Scandalously, it was her eighth buggy, now. The eighth buggy that father Raber had bought for her, never speaking a word to her about her driving. He just bought her new rigs whenever she needed them. He had never refused her. Everyone knew the stories of Abigail Raber's pacer.

Of course, one could expect a buggy to last only a short while in the hands of a spirited Amish lad. Light racing buggies and fast horses harnessed to rambunctious boys—and of course a buggy could be run into the ground in a very short time, indeed. But a lass of twenty-nine was thought to be a different matter altogether, and it had been a topic of no small gossip in the District that Herman Raber Sr. had spoiled his daughter with an endless supply of buggies, and with a racing steed to match her spirited soul.

It was also not news in those parts that Abigail Raber had a joy of driving fast, sometimes even at night when it was most dangerous, sometimes in broad daylight, as if she were flaunting it about. As if she were wanting to be seen. As if her scar allowed her an extra measure of imprudence, an extra privilege of nonconformity. Indeed, it was widely held that Abigail Raber had managed to acquire the only traffic ticket for speeding that could be remembered among the Amish. And it was rumored to be a sport among the sheriff's deputies, trying to catch the fearless Abigail Raber in her buggy.

True, as the gossip went, Raber Sr. had derived intense satisfaction from buying the lightest rigs for Abigail. To be sure, they had all been proper in every aspect of style and form. Black with no add-on frills other than a triangular reflector on the back flap. They had also been swift as the wind. Each of the eight rigs lighter and faster than the last, custom built to his demanding specifications.

Her horse, too, was a perfect match to her spirit. It was a championship pacer that Raber had arranged to buy in Delaware, Ohio, after one of the Little Brown Jug races there. Raber had set an extravagant limit, and he had sent the purchasing agent with instructions to buy the finest of the lot. Though the price was severe, Herman Raber Sr. had not been disappointed. In the years since, Abigail's pacer had run the wheels off eight buggies and showed no signs of tiring in front of Abigail's enthusiastic whip.

But today, Abigail had left home with her baskets and had driven slowly to her stand. She needed the length of an entire day. Needed to speak with Cal Troyer face to face. To convince him.

Though her prices were set at triple the going rate, none of the sisters would know anything other than that she had set up to sell baskets beside the road, and likely, as usual, she'd not be home until they all had sold. So, with a buggy loaded to over-filling, she had walked her anxious pacer north to Route 250. Outside of Mt. Eaton, she stopped at a phone booth and called Cal Troyer at his church house. Then, east of Mt. Eaton on 250, she had set up to sell and to wait until Troyer would be able to meet her. The trouble was, even at triple the going rates, most of her baskets had sold before noon.

She gathered up the last five, arranged them in the grass in front of her table, and sat back down to count her profits. Seven hundred and eighty-seven tax-free dollars from something like twenty dollars of unwoven New York City art-supply reeds.

The challenge now was to not sell the last five. Once they were gone, she would have no reason to tarry beside the road. No reason to be there when Cal Troyer arrived. She stepped around to the front of her table, took one of the largest baskets, and sat back down to unravel the reeds. When she had the bas-ket about half undone, she set it on the table without its price tag, content that she'd never be able to sell out, now, before Cal could break away from his morning's obligations in the city.

When she was down to only two baskets, Cal arrived in his pickup. He parked on a side road, came over to her, kneeled down beside her table at the edge of the grass, and listened as she told him the details of her conversation with David in their cabin the night before. She told Troyer of the promises Hawkins had made to return to her at the end of next week on terms her father could accept. She told Cal Troyer of the vow that Hawkins had made that she would always have a life joined to his. Most of all, she hoped that whatever Hawkins intended to do, Cal Troyer could see, now, that it surely would not be murder. She hoped that Troyer would understand it all, in those simple terms, and then convince the sheriff that Hawkins was not a threat to anyone at all. That Hawkins was not the murderer of Eric Bromfield and would not become the murderer of Jesse Sands.

Cal listened to all she had to say and then returned to Millersburg. Abigail sat at her table with her last, half-unwoven basket and labored to assure herself that she had done the right thing. She tried to convince herself that the pure logic of it was irrefutable. But she also wrestled, now, with a lingering suspicion that Cal Troyer was no longer so convinced of the peaceful intentions of David Hawkins.

Until last night, no one had seen David since his night trip to the jail. But now she had seen him. She had talked to him. She had held him in the cabin. She knew that Sheriff Robertson need no longer hunt for him. Knew that the man who had kissed her, loved her, held her—that that man had not killed anyone. That he had not murdered Eric Bromfield, and, assuredly, now would not kill Jesse Sands. She knew it as one who knows a lover, with a lover's conviction, with a lover's hope.

It made such perfect sense in the only terms that Abigail Raber could understand. It made such an absolutely reasonable truth. The burden of revenge was a lifetime's staggering weight. To seek revenge and to act upon that worldly impulse could bring only a worse fate. To kill for revenge would do as much damage to the soul of a killer as it did to the life of a victim. To strike in violence was forbidden. Even to respond in kind to a threat was forbidden. The life of peace was the only way to heaven. There were good and fast reasons to cling steadfastly to pacifism. There were also scriptures that put retribution out of the reach of the Peaceful Ones. The Plain People knew from their lives of martyrdom in Europe that the violence of resistance multiplied itself a dozen times over to the detriment of all. So, in Abigail's world, the thought of vengeance was as foreign as the thought of war.

But she also lived in the world. Separate from it, that was true, but in the world nevertheless. And she knew that in the world, the violence of men seemed to rule the day. The influence of evil seemed to poison their minds. The preachers were right. The ways of the English were inscrutable. Their lives seemed to hang from a puppeteer's strings, and the puppeteer cherished violence and destruction. The English willingly walked the broad road to destruction.

But surely not David Hawkins. He knew the narrow way. He knew the staggering burden of needless bloodshed. She had told him in the cabin, and he had agreed. So surely now, Cal Troyer could also see. David Hawkins had left the broad way and had chosen the narrow way to life. David Hawkins was one of the peaceful ones. He was to be her husband.

With contentment, knowing that she had done all that she could, Abigail pulled the last unfinished basket into her lap and idly began to weave the reeds back into place. Her fingers handled the task from memory. The long ends began to disappear into the basket, and Abigail began happily to consider the route she'd take home with her racer.

When the basket was nearly finished, she ducked under a wooden fence at the edge of a pasture and whistled her pacer to her side. She reached up, stroked between his ears, and then led him to her buggy under a tree. She hitched him, walked him around to the table beside the road, and wrapped the reins under the corner of a large foundation stone that she had long ago hauled there for the purpose of tethering her horse.

As she prepared to gather her chair and grocery bag into the back of the buggy, a station wagon with out-of-town plates sped by, pulled in with a skid beyond, and backed up to her table on the gravel berm. An English lady in a long, flowered, low-cut summer dress got out and ushered three small children from the back seat of the station wagon.

"Look, kids," she said. "She's weaving one now."

The mother pushed her unwilling children up to the stand and asked Abigail, "Did you learn to do that from your grandmother?"

Abigail smiled openly and remembered how she had learned to weave her simple baskets from a book at the library. She said, "A bit, I suppose," circumspectly, and finished up the basket.

She penciled on a price that was fully six times that of any similar basket in Holmes County, and by the time the family had loaded the last of her baskets into the back of their station wagon, she was headed home with all of her baskets sold to tourists, and $1,289 in her little cloth purse.

18

THAT same morning, as Cal Troyer was taking the call from Abigail, Branden returned to the Hawkins place on the west edge of town. He went in through the side door off the drive-way, opened the back room in the basement, and took down the logbook where Hawkins had recorded the data for his rifle cartridges. At the point where Hawkins had made his most re-cent entry, Branden read the lot number again and then searched the shelves below the workbench for the ammo can that held the 6 mm rounds. Finding the right can, he set it on the bench, pulled up the top of the can, and heard the watertight gasket release its seal. Inside the can, he found seven plastic boxes of ammo fitted with individual spacers to separate the single rounds, each of the boxes labeled with a lot number. He set the seven boxes out on the workbench and began the task of match-ing them to the records in the logbooks. The seven boxes of 6 mm rifle ammo had been recorded in three different logs over the past two years. None of the boxes listed there matched the lot number of the cartridges Hawkins had described only a few days earlier, as the last entry in his book. Hawkins's last box of cartridges was missing.

Branden lifted a cartridge out of its slot, replaced the boxes in the can, and returned the can to its shelf under the loading bench. He put back all of the logbooks except the one that held the data for the last rounds Hawkins had made. Then he locked up, pulled out of the drive, and drove to a small gun shop in the hills north of town.

The shop was in an old converted garage at the side of a one-story frame house, set back in the woods at the end of a long gravel drive. As Branden entered the shop-garage, Billy Martin, dressed in surplus army green, came in through a door from the adjoining house with a mug of coffee and took his place behind the counter.

Branden asked, "What do you make of that?" and set the cartridge on the counter.

Martin looked the cartridge over and said, "A 6 mm PPC."

Branden showed him the log entry. Martin studied the data and said, "It's a benchrest competition round."

"Strictly target, Billy?"

"Right. Where'd you get hold of it?"

"Could you hunt with it?" Branden asked.

"No point, I reckon," Martin said. "22-250s are better for groundhogs and that's about all a 6 mm PPC is any good for, other than punching holes in paper."

"It's strictly a target round?" Branden asked again.

The shop owner nodded yes and said, "Benchrest target shooting."

"Could it kill a man?" Branden asked pointedly.

Martin turned back to a shelf behind his counter and pulled down a book. He leafed through the pages and found data on the 6 mm PPC cartridge. He studied several tables of numbers, and said, "From 100 yards, the 75 grain 6 mm PPC bullet, traveling at 3,400 feet per second at the muzzle, packs 1,550 foot-pounds of energy. At 200 yards, it drops to 1,240 foot-pounds."

"Would that kill a man?"

"It could, but it's not likely."

"What would make it more likely?"

"Maybe a head shot." He looked curiously at Branden, a bit nervous.

"From 300 yards?" Branden asked.

"Maybe even 400, Doc, but who's gonna make a head shot at that range?"

Branden thanked him, pocketed the cartridge, took the logbook, and drove back to the Hawkins place. In the secret basement room, he replaced the cartridge, slipped the book back into its slot on the shelves, and turned to the door. On impulse, he pushed the door shut from the inside and confronted the empty pegs where the composite target rifle once had hung. For some elusive reason that he thought only briefly strange, the professor realized he was not surprised. Hawkins had taken his bullets and his rifle.

When he stepped out of the side door of the Hawkins house, Branden found Ricky Niell in uniform, leaning back against the professor's light truck. Niell's cruiser blocked the drive.

"This time I'll need to know what you're doing here, Professor," Niell said officially.

Branden briefly considered giving Niell an evasive answer but gauged it was time to start figuring David Hawkins on terms Cal Troyer was incapable of accepting. However reasonable his conviction that Hawkins had not murdered Eric Bromfield, there was still the matter of Jesse Sands and Hawkins's revenge. Whatever game Bruce Robertson was playing, it was clear the sheriff still intended for him and Cal to keep looking for Hawkins too. Branden had no intentions, now, of falling off the Hawkins trail. He had come here to check on one of Caroline's hunches. And now he knew it was true. David Hawkins had taken possession of both his rifle and his ammunition, and that struck Branden as the pivotal fact in the case so far.

He turned, unlocked the side door, and led Niell, without comment, into the basement. As he worked the hidden switch to throw the bolts on the inside of the door to the back room, Niell seemed unsurprised.

When Branden let Niell into the room, Niell drew in a startled breath and turned slowly in place, saying, "My God!" Once his surprise ebbed he said, "We knew that Hawkins was in a Special Forces Unit, but this is something else altogether."

Branden appreciated Niell's dismay. He let a moment pass and quietly asked, "Do you know what Hawkins did, specifically?"

"Sniper," Niell said, sounding chilled.

Branden smiled weakly and shook his head, acknowledging that Robertson would have checked. He took a seat on a tall wooden stool next to the workbench, and then glanced at the door and decided not to mention the missing rifle.

"We figured it'd be too much," Niell said, "for Hawkins to have given up all of his firearms entirely."

"From what Cal says, Ricky, that's pretty much what he intends to do. Sell off his collection and make the change."

"Go Amish, you mean?" Ricky asked.

Branden nodded.

"Then you don't believe Hawkins killed Bromfield?" Ricky asked.

"Cal doesn't. I'm not so sure anymore."

"And Sands? Do you figure he'll try for Sands?" Niell asked.

"From what I've seen here, yes," Branden said. "Do you know why Hawkins taped that note to Sands's jail cell window?"

"Robertson thinks he was playing with Sands. Messing with his head," Niell said. His expression said he didn't totally agree with the sheriff.

Outside as they locked up, Niell said, "Robertson knows that Eric Bromfield had learned something in New Jersey. Something Bromfield never got to tell Marty Holcombe. Robertson made some phone calls to the prison where Sands did his time. We know that's where Bromfield went. At least it's one of the places Bromfield went. But Robertson didn't get any help from the warden. And he's not planning to follow up."

Branden mulled that over for a moment and asked, "Do you know why not?"

"The sheriff thinks that by Friday next week, we'll all have heard more than we're likely to want from David Hawkins. Robertson's decided to wait him out."

Branden stood in a narrow strip of shade beside the white house and thought. It wouldn't be Robertson's way to just sit around and "wait him out." Not unless he had decided that searching further for David Hawkins would be entirely futile. Not unless Robertson had decided, based on what he had discovered, that David Hawkins would never be found until David Hawkins himself decided to permit it.

"Is Bruce down at the jail?" Branden asked.

Niell shook his head and said, "Columbus. He's got a Buckeye Sheriff's Association Meeting, until tomorrow."

"Who's on duty tonight at the jail?"

"I am," Ricky said. "Me and Phil Schrauzer."

"Ricky, I need to talk with Jesse Sands."

Niell shook his head, smiled, and said, "And what makes you think I'm gonna allow that to happen again?"

Branden pulled himself into the cab of his truck, shut the door, rolled down the window, looked at Niell, and said, "Because, Deputy, you're like me. You figure the truth is somewhere between Cal Troyer and Bruce Robertson. That's why you told me about New Jersey just now."

19

HE lingered in the upstairs closet for an hour, after Branden and Niell had left. That had been the prudent thing to do, considering that Branden was the only person who might figure it out in time. There was no point tipping his hand to the one man who could surely stop him.

If necessary, he'd have waited in that closet until midnight. He had come too far. He had waited too long. He knew the true nature of justice, and he intended to have it on his terms, not theirs. He'd never again accept the pathetic, so-called justice of a nation of cowards, weaklings, and traitors.

His right hand still held the grip of his .45 automatic, but the bulk of its lovely, reassuring weight was taken by the shoulder holster. It was a stainless steel Smith and Wesson model 645, better, he thought, than the third-generation 4506. He would never risk it here, but the temptation to take it out had been profound, an almost irresistible impulse to work a few rounds through the chamber. The slide was honed to whisper smoothness, and the trigger was satin. If only he could palm the rounds, he had thought, maybe a few dry snaps of the hammer would calm him.

The new silencer for the Browning Buckmark was parked in its black leather sleeve, strapped to his thigh with Velcro ties. The sleeve was made of good leather, from a batch he had saved from his days as a Boy Scout. Easy to strap it in place with the Velcro, just below the slit in his front pants pocket. It rode there on his thigh, safely out of view, ever ready. Too bad, really, to have lost the Ruger .22. It was just too wonderfully accurate. The silencer was mated to it as if it were an integral part of the barrel. It released little more than a whisper. The Ruger always performed. It had never jammed. He knew it'd print on a target inside a half-inch circle at 25 yards.

But the Browning seemed better, now, lighter. The Ruger had always stabbed its metallic weight into his kidneys. The target barrel was heavy, and the slide knurls annoyed the skin at his lower back. Why hadn't he taken the Browning out earlier? So much lighter; so much more comfortable.

Earlier, when those two had been in the basement, he had brought out the Browning and its silencer. The rush had been nearly overpowering as he had screwed the two together. He had slipped the safety off, and had moved into place on the landing at the top of the basement stairs.

It would have been so easy at the top of the steps. Just wait for them on the landing, and then be rid of them both. If either of them moved after he had dropped them, then two more rounds into the back of the skull. No noise, little blood, and Millersburg would have two more murders that the Sheriff would never understand. What a joke. Robertson still hadn't comprehended the murder of the reporter.

Moving out of the closet, however, had been a colossal mistake. He admitted that to himself, now. Better think about that later, he whispered in the dark. Another poor decision. One more could ruin him.

Don't kid yourself, he thought morosely. You're losing the touch. Ten years ago, such a blunder would have been unthinkable.

20

Wednesday, June 11
9:00 P.M.

JESSE Sands lay on a cot in his isolated, second-floor cell and scornfully blew smoke toward the ceiling. His fingers were clasped behind his head, elbows up, his cigarette hanging loose at his lips. The sleeves of his orange inmate's pullover were rolled up tight onto the rounds of his shoulders. The tattoos on his biceps looked faded in the dim, smoky light of his cell.

Inside the cell, Sands's public defender lawyer, Jack Crawford, sat on a straight chair with his briefcase open on his knees. Branden and Niell stood on the other side of the bars.

"I have advised my client," Crawford said, "to say nothing to either of you."

"You're wasting your time, Crawford," Niell said.

"You're due in court, Niell," Crawford said. "Violating my client's civil rights the last time you brought someone here to talk to Mr. Sands."

Niell scoffed. "What's the difference to you, Sands?" Niell said. "We're going to tie you up with at least three murders, anyway. Next week only counts for Janet Hawkins."

"You don't have to say anything, Jesse," Crawford said.

"Well, Deputy," Sands said, mocking a country accent. "I just don't know what I'm gonna tell you. Don't have nothing to say, and that's pretty much all she wrote." He sat up on the edge of his cot, crushed the cigarette on the floor, picked up the butt, and flipped it insolently at Niell.

Branden turned, walked back into the upstairs hallway, and took a wooden chair back into the cellblock. He put it down gently in front of Sands's cell and sat down next to Niell, who still stood in front of the bars. Then the professor stretched his legs out beside the bars as if he had nothing better to do on a lazy spring night. He sat there for nearly twenty minutes without speaking. Sands lay on his cot, smoking. Niell pulled the door open on the vacant cell across from Sands and sat down on the cot, legs hanging over, back propped against the bars. Sands stepped to his toilet, relieved himself, and sat back on his bed.

"They say you robbed that kid in the buggy the night you came into Millersburg," Branden said.

"You're a fool, Professor," Sands said. "Go home."

"You held a gun to the head of the most peaceful soul on earth, and you think me a fool?" Branden ridiculed.

"You're a fool and so was he."

"The sheriff thinks one of those Amish 'fools' is getting ready to kill you, Sands," Branden said.

Sands scoffed and said, "Right."

"What if he's right?" Branden asked.

"He's not," Sands said with confidence and composure.

"Then tell me why he's not," Branden said without looking into Sands's cell.

"You don't get it and neither does the Fat Man," Sands said, bored now with the matter. "Get out. I'm sleepy."

"I can walk out of here any time I choose," Branden said.

"Get out, you bore me," Sands said and stretched on his cot.

"Why did you kill her, Sands?"

"She was there."

"Shut up, Sands," Crawford snapped.

Sands gave him the finger.

"Why Millersburg?" Branden asked.

"It was on my way."

"Why's he after you?"

"He has always . . . " Sands stopped abruptly and cursed himself under his breath.

"Who has?" Branden asked.

Sands kept quiet. Niell listened intently from across the aisle, but, beyond breathing normally, he moved not so much as a fraction of an inch.

"Who has what?" Branden asked.

Sands glared at the ceiling.

"He has always what?"

Sands rolled over and closed his eyes.

"What has he always done, and who is it that has always done it, Sands?" Branden asked and then sat quietly for another few minutes.

Eventually, on impulse, Branden asked the principal question again. "What did you tell David Hawkins the night he came here as an Amishman to forgive you for killing his daughter?"

"Again," Crawford said, shaking his head, "I advise you to say nothing, Mr. Sands."

But Sands answered anyway, taunting Branden. "I told him that I pulled the trigger, but I wasn't the one who actually killed his daughter."

21

Friday, June 13
7:00 A.M.

AS soon as Robertson was due back in town, Branden arrived
at the jail and waited for Robertson in the sheriff's corner office.
Ellie Troyer let him in with her keys and went back out to her
counter to make a pot of coffee. While the night dispatcher
finished his shift, Ellie sat with Branden and waited. Branden
could tell from her questions that Ricky Niell had kept her well
informed on matters of Jesse Sands.

"Do you have it figured out, what Sands meant by saying
'He has always . . .'?" Ellie asked the professor over her first
mug of coffee. She was parked in the sheriff's big desk chair.

"No, does Niell?" Branden asked and smiled at her near-
Mennonite transparency. At the way she had plainly and simply come straight to the point.

Ellie Troyer liked working on what she called the "good side"
of people. She especially liked anyone who would stand up to
Bruce Robertson, and these days, that most particularly included
Professor Branden, and Ricky Niell. And if she could manage
it, she planned that things would fall out on her shift, to Niell's
benefit. And so today, she pushed a little harder on the professor as he slouched in the leather chair beside Robertson's cherry
desk.

His back was low on the cushion. His legs stuck out straight, ankles crossed. His elbows were perched on the armrests, and his hands were folded in his lap. His wavy brown hair was combed neatly into place. His beard was trimmed close. Ellie studied him a moment longer, shuffled Robertson's stack of mail around on the sheriff's desk, and then continued.

"Ricky hasn't figured what it means, either," she said, and swung the chair to the side. She got up and walked over to gaze at the arm patches on Robertson's wall.

Branden asked, "Do you think Sands actually meant he did not kill Janet Hawkins?"

Ellie was dressed in a long, light green dress, with a high white collar. Her hair was tied in a bun, not so much as a matter of style, but because she had been out late with Ricky Niell, and there hadn't been time to attend to it. Her reading glasses hung from a lanyard around her neck. Her shoes were simple black loafers. All in all, she could have added a prayer bonnet and almost fooled a tourist out on the square into thinking she was surely Amish. Maybe Mennonite, or something like that. Few tourists ever bothered to learn the difference. Branden pulled himself up a bit in his chair and waited for Ellie to give her answer.

"He probably meant that there is something about that murder that nobody has figured out yet," Ellie said.

Branden quietly nodded his agreement.

Ellie sat back down in Robertson's chair and finished the last sip of her coffee. Before she could get up, they heard Robertson's voice out in the hall. Ellie got herself out of the chair quickly, pushed it back up under the desk, winked at Branden, and rushed to the credenza where Robertson's coffeepot was kept. As Robertson plowed into the room, she was scooping fresh grounds into the empty basket of the coffee maker.

Robertson held up a full cup of coffee, laughed knowingly at Ellie's deception, and said, "You know I get my first cup outside, young lady." He set his briefcase upright on his desk, sat on the corner nearest Branden, and frowned. "Why have you been annoying the professor, Ellie?"

Ellie feigned hurt feelings, smiled mischievously, and stepped out to her dispatcher's desk.

Robertson sat on the corner of his desk, opened the latches on his briefcase, took out a CD, and said, "Mike, you've got to hear this song." He stepped around to the player on the shelves behind his desk, slid in the disk, punched up the song, and hit play. "I got this down in Columbus," Robertson said, and dropped into the chair behind his desk.

Branden asked, "Is that Ian Tyson?"

Robertson said, "Who else?" and held a finger up to his lips.

Tyson's strong voice gave out a proud, waltzing ballad about a horse named Stormy who had saved a mother and her baby. Robertson sang along at one point, with his eyes shut, arms waving in the air with the beat:

> "Old Stormy just snorted,
> and he hit that long trot.
> Man how that pony could give 'er."

When the ballad was over, Robertson spun around, snapped the music off, and said, "Man, that's good. Where do they get those songs?"

Branden asked, "The horse saved the day?"

"You weren't listening?" Robertson asked, disbelieving.

"I suppose so," Branden said weakly, struggling not to laugh.

Robertson turned and caught Branden's helpless expression. "That horse is a hero!" he said, exasperated.

Branden tried to redeem himself by saying, "OK, Bruce, I'll bite. Why do you like that song?"

Robertson sat down heavily and said, "Cowboy songs are about life, Mike. Philosophy. Maybe it's just too deep for you college boys up on the hill."

"Why don't you try me," Branden said, amused and softly laughing at his petty sin.

Robertson forgave him instantly, and warmed quickly and enthusiastically to the task. "That's a song about competence, Mike. The kind of raw competence that flat gets the job done, when nobody else can do it. One horse that could have made that ride. One man who had the guts to try. Ability, Mike, and can-do pride."

"And you like that?" Branden asked, knowing full well that steadfastness and strong ability were among the few things in life that Robertson truly honored.

Robertson turned philosophical. "They say you're supposed to be happy, Mike, but I don't have the faintest idea what that means any more. Not since Renie died. On the radio last night, driving back from Columbus, there was some dope with a talk show, squawkin' about how we're meant to be happy people. Do this, do that, be good to yourself, be happy. Happiness? I wouldn't know what that is."

Branden stood, leaned against the wall by the big window, and listened, aware that Robertson rarely emptied himself so openly.

"Now, satisfaction is something I can understand." Robertson lit a cigarette and drew on it with obvious enjoyment. "I'm talking about the ability to do the job, regardless of circumstances. Like you, up on the Marblehead point, with Ricky Niell's life in your hands. I'd have given a year's pay to have seen you. Like Stormy, there, who never let down.

"So, if you ask me what pulls my chain, I'd have to say it is ability, Mike, and competence. Also steadfastness, loyalty, endurance. People who'll stand in the gap when their moment arrives. Also liberty, justice, and trustworthiness. But happiness? Don't rightly know what that is, Mike. I'd rather be competent, these days, than happy. I'd sooner be thought vigilant. So, in that little cowboy song, there, I get all of that. Stormy, the only one who could make it through to town, when it needed doing the most."

Branden acknowledged his friend with a nod, folded his arms, and gazed out the window for a few moments without speaking. Robertson shuffled papers on his desk and blushed slightly. Branden said, "OK, let's hear it again," and sat down beside Robertson's desk to listen.

Robertson stalled a moment, and then seemed pleased. He wheeled around and punched play again, and they listened to the ballad of Stormy the mighty bronc, out on the Milk River Ridge.

Branden heard it through and remembered the playgrounds after school. Even then, Bruce Robertson had managed unquenchable spells of soaring enthusiasm and exhilaration. He could still be that way, even now. Then, too, there had been the downward spirals into depression, when Robertson would seem to topple into an abyss of untouchable gloom. He was the most changeable and also the most personable man the professor had ever considered a friend. The only other one who could equal the rotund sheriff in steadfastness, loyalty, and trustworthiness was Cal Troyer. And when the professor had found the one woman who was the equal of these two in heart and soul, he had married her.

But something important in Bruce had died with Irene Cotton. Somehow he had lost his hold on one of the capacities of life. Cal was tangled in it, Branden knew. Cal had sat with her in the hospital as she lay dying. Bruce, however, despite his love for her, perhaps even because of it, hadn't allowed himself to understand how gravely ill she had been, and he had been out working a case when she died. Now, Branden realized, most of the real trouble between Cal and Bruce arose from the guilt that had torn a corner loose in the sheriff's big heart.

"Bruce, I want to talk to you about Cal."

"What's there to say?" Robertson said, suddenly grouchy.

"I think there's more to the murders of Janet Hawkins and Eric Bromfield than you've let on."

"Hawkins did the Bromfield kid," Robertson said, "and he's setting up for Sands. Cal knows where Hawkins is, and he's not talking. If Sands takes a bullet, I'm going to arrest Cal Troyer as an accomplice to murder."

"Even Sands, himself, doesn't think Hawkins is gunning for him."

Robertson shot back, "You've talked to Jesse Sands?" He knew that Branden had, but had planned to use such a moment to squeeze Branden hard when he had him on the defensive.

It didn't work. Branden understood the transaction instinctively and coolly said, "You know I have, Bruce. Niell would have told you."

Robertson looked smug and said, "And I told Niell to let you in to see Sands if you ever asked."

Branden stood again, stretched his legs, and ambled over to one of the north windows looking out on Courthouse Square. As he watched pedestrians in the square, he asked, "Then don't you think Sands could have meant something important by telling Hawkins that someone else actually had killed his daughter?"

Robertson pushed himself away from the desk, got up, and walked over to the coffeepot that Ellie had left on the credenza, and said, "Look, Mike, this is a simple case." He stepped out of the office and came back directly with a carafe of water. As he poured it into the top of the coffee maker, he said, "You've been all over this case, and so have we. Janet Hawkins was killed because she was in the wrong place at the wrong time. True, it was her own home, but still she was in the wrong place. Bromfield was killed because he knew the wrong thing. True, it was his job, but he still knew the wrong thing. The things he knew about Hawkins would have tipped us off to what Hawkins intends for Sands." He snapped the switch on the coffeepot, and added, "It's as simple as that, Mike, and you know it."

"Then why do I feel that none of that can be right?" Branden asked from his spot in front of the window.

"Beats the tar out of me," Robertson said, and sat back down behind his desk.

"You think all we can do is wait it out?" Branden asked.

"That's what I'm going to do," Robertson said as he sorted and opened his mail. "Guards around the clock. Move Sands over to the courthouse ahead of schedule. Hold him there until his trial starts. Stay awake and ready until the judge pronounces sentence. When Sands has been turned over to the state penal authorities, I'll be able to work the Bromfield murder the way it deserves."

"Sands goes to trial next Friday?"

"Right."

"There's nothing scheduled before then?"

"Like what?"

"I don't know. Maybe he needs a doctor."

"He doesn't."

"Any other trials before that one?"

"None that involve me. If it weren't for Sands and that Greyson thing, I'd be on vacation," Robertson said.

"What Greyson thing?" Branden asked and turned from the window.

"The mayor wants a little ceremony next Wednesday morning to give Greyson a commendation. 'Retired guard captures felon'—that sort of thing."

"A commendation."

"Courthouse steps, next Wednesday morning, at nine."

"And that's all you've got coming up on your calendar?"

"Thought I might move Sands to a north-facing cell so he can watch Greyson," Robertson said, sarcasm mixed with grim satisfaction.

"Have you talked with Greyson at all?" Branden asked.

"Once or twice. He's washed up," Robertson said offhand. "Too many nights walking a beat. Mike, give it up."

As Branden walked out of the red-brick jailhouse, he thought to himself that likely he would do just that. Give it up. Wait it out like Robertson. And he would, he told himself, soon enough. Just as soon as he had nosed around the three places Robertson had neglected to push for answers. Uncharacteristically, Robertson had left three strings dangling. First, there was the girlfriend of Eric Bromfield. Robertson hadn't mentioned her, but Marty Holcombe had. Then there was the rifle range where David Hawkins had won his marksmanship trophy. Last, there was New Jersey, where Eric Bromfield seemed to have uncovered something notable the day before he came home. The day before he had taken three .22 slugs to the head.

22

Friday, June 13
11:00 A.M.

NANCY Blain bent over to the viewfinder on her black Nikon camera and studied the image of a wagonload of boisterous Amish kids rolling along in the distance behind two stolid Belgians. She touched a light finger to the focus ring atop the long zoom, and fired off a string of shots as the wagon turned into a lane in front of a large Amish farmstead. After the motor drive had fallen silent, she held her eye to the viewfinder a while longer, pulled the lens up toward a strip-planted field of hay and corn, and refocused on a fence line at the far edge of the field.

"We were lovers," she said at last. "We were going to get married."

The short sleeves of her T-shirt were rolled up high on her arms. Her black jeans were fashionable, and beltless. Her worn and scuffed hiking boots could recently have come off the Blue Ridge trail. Her dark blue Cleveland Indians road hat was turned around backwards, and her black hair was cut severely short. She stood back from the camera's tripod, turned around, and looked at the professor sadly.

"Eric was a great guy. About the greatest guy you could find these days. We met in college."

"At Ohio University?"

She nodded yes and turned back to her camera. A high, white cloud drifted across the tranquil sky and shaded the hill where her lens was focused. Contrast and light seemed good to her, and she took a shot of the corn that ran in swirling rows, up to the fence line on top of the rise. The soft, arching rows of green led the eyes to the sharp, horizontal line of wire, and from that border, the gaze ascended into a gentle blue sky, patched out to the horizon in every direction with lumbering puffs of white.

Branden sat in the grass on the bank beside the tripod, knees pulled up to his chest. "Marty Holcombe says Eric phoned him the night he was coming home from New Jersey."

She popped a pair of sunglasses over her eyes, sat down close to him on the bank, and looked out over the Amish valley. Then she turned to him, and intently said, "He called Holcombe, Professor, but he didn't call me. We had a date the next night." She fell silent.

Eventually, Branden said, "There's a nice shot of a manure spreader," and pointed toward the saddle between two planted hills.

"I've got a thousand of those," Nancy said offhandedly.

"One would think you'd have plenty of all of these shots on file," Branden said circumspectly.

"Marty wants fresh shots for a feature. Warrior turns Amish —Hawkins, before and after. The mystery man of Holmes County. Turned in his swords for a plow."

"So Holcombe's going to run Bromfield's stories about Hawkins?"

"Wouldn't you?" she asked, surprised.

"I don't know," Branden said. "I really don't know."

"Well, he's not going to print them until after the trial, because that's the way Robertson wants it. But they'll run in three parts when Sands is gone."

She lifted her ball cap, ran a flat palm over her short hair, and replaced the cap. Her light skin sparkled with a sheen of perspiration. The sun came out from under the cloud and hit them there on the little bank near the gravel road. She turned her cap around frontways and pulled the visor down low over her eyes. Then she lay back in the grass, crossed her legs, and locked her fingers behind her head. Eventually she sat up and studied the little valley where her camera was aimed. Then she stood up abruptly. "Looks like I'm done here, Professor. Heading back in."

Branden stood, brushed off the seat of his jeans, and asked, "Have you read any of Eric's stories?"

"All of them. Each draft, every version," she said. She lifted the Nikon off the tripod, unscrewed the zoom lens, fished a cap out of her front jeans pocket, and fit it onto the camera body. She carried the two pieces back to her red Bronco. As she bent over in the back seat to stow the gear, Nancy said, "I can't believe he's really gone." Then she straightened up, glanced at Branden, and walked to the tripod. "He had me read all his stuff before he gave it to Holcombe."

"Why?"

"Because Eric was a lousy writer. I scrubbed his copy before he let anyone read it."

"You didn't mind?"

"We were a team. I read all of his papers in college, too. Normally, he couldn't have written his way out of a paper bag." She teared up a little in the corners of her eyes, and explained, "I liked helping him, OK?"

Branden lifted a camera bag and carried it to the Bronco. "Could anything in those stories have been a reason for Hawkins to have killed him?"

She opened the driver's door and climbed up. She started the engine and rolled down the electric windows. Branden stepped around to the passenger's side, dropped the bag onto the front seat, and leaned in toward her. "I need to know what Eric knew that wasn't in those stories."

She shut the engine down and stretched her arms straight out against the steering wheel. After a few seconds thinking, she relaxed her arms and said, "There's nothing in them that Hawkins can have been worried about. Besides, didn't most of his friends already know?"

Branden acknowledged that wordlessly and said, "Eric must have gotten hold of something he wasn't supposed to know."

She shrugged and asked, "Like what?"

Branden pushed back from the Bronco and came around to her side. "Can you tell me where Eric went to get his story?"

"All over."

"Like where?"

"I know he went to New Jersey."

"Do you know why?"

"Jesse Sands."

"Prison?"

"Right. Also to Fort Benning."

"That's a new one."

"The Special Forces sniper teams train there. It's called the U.S. Army Marksmanship Training Unit. Did you know Hawkins was an instructor?"

"No."

"Well, Eric went to Fort Benning and got that angle. It's part of the story Holcombe's waiting to run."

"Anywhere else?"

"D.C."

"Why?"

"The Vietnam Memorial, and to check on things at the Veteran's Administration."

"Did he get anything there?"

"Not really. Hawkins just up and quit the forces one day, and walked away. Two years later he showed up in Millersburg. The VA tried to contact him about a pension, but he turned them away for the first year or so."

"Then where'd Eric go next?"

"Last I had heard, he was in New Jersey."

"Marty says he got a call from Eric that night."

"Like I said, Professor, Marty did, and I didn't." She started the engine again. "The way he tells it, Eric had something new that changed the whole Hawkins matter. But what it was, I honestly couldn't tell you."

After she had driven off, Branden sat on the little grassy rise and gazed out across the valley. The lad with the manure spreader had his team headed back to the barns for another load. The wagon of kids had emptied out onto the front lawn at an Amish house, where they bounced, in their long dresses and little vests, on a giant trampoline. A lady in a dark purple dress and black bonnet was hanging a line of clothes behind her house. The colors hung straight in the quiet afternoon sun. Lilac, surf turquoise, lavender, rose, aqua, and a gentle mauve.

The puzzle of David Hawkins grew in Branden's mind. He had been at the top of his form. An instructor at Fort Benning. Then one day he had walked away from it all.

So, something must have happened in the two years that followed. Maybe something had happened earlier, and it had just taken two years for Hawkins to sort it out. But something had drawn him to Cal Troyer. He had set himself up on the west edge of town to live the quiet life. But, as Cal had said, that had not been enough for Hawkins. He had sought the extreme withdrawal from the world that only an Amish life could provide. He had embraced Amish thought, Amish life, and Amish restrictions, carrying his penance a step further than most. He'd hung up his guns and promised himself to an Amish family. Promised himself, on Amish terms, to the Amish ways. Promised himself to an Amish beauty of twenty-nine, who carried her life's scars on her cheek.

Gradually, Branden realized that there were only two ways for this all to end. Two extreme possibilities, with no middle ground, and no compromise. The dilemma that Hawkins faced could be defined in only those two ways, one the complete antithesis of the other. If what Robertson was saying was true, Hawkins was going to kill Jesse Sands, and in doing that, he would destroy the one thing in life that he had spent his last seven years searching after fervently. On the other hand, if Cal Troyer was right, this case had nothing whatsoever to do with the revenge of David Hawkins on Jesse Sands. And if that was true, then why had Hawkins prepared a 6 mm PPC load? Why had he taken his long-range rifle down off its secret basement hooks? What had Eric Bromfield discovered in New Jersey? Finally, if Cal was right and not Robertson, then why hadn't David Hawkins made an appearance anywhere in Holmes County since the day Abigail Raber had found a pistol wrapped in blankets in the back of Hawkins's buggy?

23

Monday, June 16

FOUR phone calls to New Jersey by Professor Branden, three by Ricky Niell ostensibly, but not entirely, under the authority of Bruce Robertson, two faxes, and six hours in the offices of bureaucrats in the penal system of that state, and after a day and a half, Mike Branden had managed to pencil his name onto the desk calendar of the warden of New Jersey State Prison. Actually, he discovered, his appointment had been only with the warden's executive secretary, and by 3:00 P.M. on Monday of the week when Jesse Sands was to come out for trial, Branden had all but given up on the hope of talking to Warden Franks.

The red-eye from Cleveland had landed early that morning in Newark. He'd rented a car from a sleepy attendant and had driven the turnpike of the Garden State with a surge of commuters as the sun came up. He had found the stone walls of the prison, circled around to the new brick front, and presented himself to the warden's office by 8:30, having slept only a little on the flight. His appointment was to have been at 9:00. Trouble was, his appointment was not with the warden, and by 10:30, the warden's executive secretary had "done all she could with Warden Franks."

"I'm sorry, Professor," she said. "I have you down on my calendar from nine until nine-fifteen. I also hope that you can appreciate that the warden cannot make himself available now, and very likely will not become available to you any time today."

She said it apologetically, but firmly, in a tone that made it clear that the words were not hers.

Branden stood in front of her desk in the large outer office and struggled to reconcile life in Millersburg with that on the East Coast. Her desk was as tidy as Arne Laughton's, president of Millersburg College, a man more familiar with the board-rooms of corporate donors than with the offices and classrooms of his professors. Branden fought a rising frustration, read the name and title on her desk for the second time, drew in a set-tling breath of slow air, and asked, "Miss Falviano, please. It's a matter of some considerable importance. Surely someone in your position of authority can help me."

She was an imposing woman who carried herself with a dig-nified air. Her clothes were expensive, a trim black suit and a white silk blouse. The brooch on her lapel hinted of old money. Her hair was tinted, with occasional lines of natural gray. Her upright posture behind her impressive desk told him she'd sat in her position for many years.

"I've got a 10:45 this Friday," she said, flipping slowly through a leather-bound scheduler on her desk. She peered up at him over the tops of her reading glasses, perched low on her nose, obvi-ously hoping that Friday would suit him. It didn't.

"I need to speak with the warden today."

A short man in all-black military attire came through the door behind Branden. Miss Falviano shifted her eyes toward him so that Branden would notice. The man in black walked past her desk without speaking, rapped twice on the warden's door, and disappeared into the office beyond.

"I'm sorry," she said, sounding as if she meant it. "Perhaps you'd be better off talking to Lieutenant Brown, anyway." As she said it, she made two little jabs with her pencil toward the door that the man in the black uniform had just entered.

Branden got her meaning, said, "I'll wait," and took a seat on one of two sofas behind a long coffee table near the front door. When Brown walked out of the warden's office, Branden followed him into the hall outside Miss Falviano's third-floor office.

"Pardon me," Branden said, and strolled up to Brown in front of the elevator.

He looked Branden over, stepped onto the elevator when the doors opened, and said, "Yes?" as he pushed the button to close the doors.

Branden followed him onto the elevator as the doors were closing and said, "My name is Mike Branden."

The lieutenant pushed impatiently on the round button marked "One" and the elevator began its descent.

"What can I do for you?" Brown asked. He hadn't really looked Branden in the eyes. Everywhere else, but not in the eyes. It was an impatient way of saying "I don't have time."

"I need to see the warden. Thought maybe you could help."

With bored resignation, Brown said, "Who's it for?"

"I don't follow."

"What case?" They stepped out of the elevator at the first floor, and Branden followed Brown out, under the canopy covering the front entrance to the prison offices. At the end of the canopy, as Brown started out into a steady drizzle toward the parking lot, Branden stopped where he was and planted his feet at the edge of the sidewalk.

Brown took several more paces and glanced back as if expecting to see just another inmate's apologist on his heels. He turned around entirely when he realized Branden was no longer there, and then came back slowly in the rain to the professor on the curb. As he walked back, Branden stood his ground and sized him up.

He was perhaps five foot-seven. His black hair was done in a military crewcut. He wore a pair of dark sunglasses in spite of the blanket of gray skies and the patter of rain on the concrete. The black trousers and shirt he wore sported several utility pockets on the thigh and the sleeves. Some closed with Velcro and others with zippers. His duty belt was made of black woven leather. There was a bulge on the outside of his right ankle where he carried a small revolver. His build was tight and powerful, and his gait was smooth. He seemed to Branden to be at once acutely aware of everything around him and unconcerned about any of it. He stopped on the pavement in front of Branden, took off his sunglasses, and said, "Is this about a parole?"

"No," Branden said, and waited.

"The parole board meets tomorrow," Brown said, by way of explanation. "I assumed you'd have some business with the warden on that."

Branden let a moment pass and then said, "We've got a little problem with one of your ex-cons back in Ohio, and I thought I had arranged a meeting with Warden Franks to talk about that."

"You've got to get past Falviano to do that."

"So I gathered."

"I'm Lieutenant Brown. Steve Brown." The lieutenant held out his hand. "I'm in charge of security matters for the warden."

Branden relaxed inwardly and shook his hand. Brown stepped up onto the curb, and suggested a dry place to talk, inside the glass and red steel doors to the prison offices.

"Anita's a buffer for the warden," Brown offered apologetically.

"Lieutenant, a sheriff's deputy in our little town did just about everything a person could do to arrange a meeting for me with Warden Franks."

"And now she's not letting you through."

Branden said, "You could say that, yes," and then "I am Professor Michael Branden. I'm here to try to figure out some things about a case we've got back home, and I think your warden has already spoken to a young reporter about this matter earlier."

"We get a lot of reporters through here," Brown answered.

"From Ohio?" Branden challenged.

Brown now seemed interested. "Not normally, but a kid did come here about two weeks ago."

"I know," Branden said. "He's dead."

Brown's eyes betrayed a surge of worry. "Jesse Sands?"

"That's the problem we've got."

"His last name was Brom-something?"

"Bromfield."

"Right. Bromfield. He's dead?" Before Branden could answer, Brown started for the elevator.

Branden followed and said, "Eric Bromfield was shot in the head on the day he returned from talking with Warden Franks."

Brown groaned audibly. He pushed the elevator button impatiently and rode up in silent thought, with Branden, to the warden's floor. In Anita Falviano's outer office, Branden hung his jacket on a coat tree inside the door. He straightened his collar and followed Brown into the warden's office. As he passed Anita Falviano's desk, he leaned a bit her way and whispered, "Thanks."

Warden Frank's office was appointed with heavy wood and thick, dark carpet. Three walls held books in walnut cases fronted with glass doors. The windows on the fourth wall were draped with heavy velvet. The corners of the room were nearly lost in shadow. A single green desk lamp was lit on the warden's black lacquer desk. Brown crossed the lavish carpet to the warden's desk and said, "Al, the Jesse Sands thing in Ohio has gone sour on us."

Warden Franks tossed a report onto the polished surface of his desk and leaned back to listen in his high-backed chair. It was upholstered in red leather, tacked with ornate brass studs. He muttered something and closed his eyes wearily.

Brown introduced Branden. Branden reconstructed the story

of Eric Bromfield's murder. The warden seemed annoyed, but Brown still seemed surprised. When Branden mentioned David Hawkins, the warden only shrugged. Branden considered that strange and then realized that, between Bromfield and Robertson, Franks would have been told the whole story of Hawkins and Bromfield. Would have been told all about Jesse Sands. It was Brown, Branden realized, who was hearing most of this for the first time. Like Robertson, Bromfield had talked only with the warden. Impressive, Branden mused, that Bromfield had managed to talk his way past Anita Falviano.

When he explained Bruce Robertson's theory of Hawkins's revenge, Branden thought he noticed Brown catching the warden's gaze with a reproachful look. When he mentioned Jesse Sands and Nabal Greyson, the warden finally stirred in his leather chair.

Warden Franks rose and took a position near one of the long velvet drapes. He pulled the heavy cloth back a few inches and watched the gray drizzle as he thought. Brown waited silently near the desk, straight and curiously rigid. Branden lowered himself into a plush chair in front of the warden's desk. The quiet in the darkened room was almost tangible. The chill, gray light of the rainy day did not penetrate the heavy curtains. Neither would the light of a sunny day. The street noises of Trenton would never reach into the warden's darkened office. Branden watched the warden at the window. Brown did too. Minutes passed.

"I don't think we're going to be able to help you, Professor," Franks said at the window and turned to face Branden. Brown rustled nervously in place beside Branden and seemed to be considering an interruption. It never came, and Brown settled back into his rigid posture.

"I wouldn't expect that you could," Branden said, "other than to help me understand what it is that Bromfield meant when he phoned his editor in Millersburg. He said he had something that changed his story entirely, and that they should hold the Sands/Hawkins story until he got back."

Brown stirred as if to answer, but Franks cut him off with a wave of his hand. "Professor," the warden said, "I don't know what that would be."

Branden said, "Warden, there's a friend of mine back in Millersburg who's got it all on the line for a fellow who looks, for all the world, as if he's preparing to make the mistake of a lifetime by killing Jesse Sands. I've got another friend, the sheriff, who'll not give a whit for his own life, if that's what it will take to put Sands on trial safely. We've already got a reporter who's dead, and the convict you released from prison has killed a young woman in her home." Impulsively, Branden added, "I'm sure you can see the downside of this, if it develops that you could have helped, and didn't."

The remark landed hard on the warden. Brown abandoned his post in front of the warden's desk and crossed the room to the windows. He drew the warden aside, and with his back turned to the professor, whispered with the warden for several minutes. Then the warden turned back to the window, and Brown turned to Branden. He said, "Professor, Bromfield talked to Billy Hershon when he was here. Hershon was the cellmate of Jesse Sands for the last eight years."

Branden asked, "There's a connection to Millersburg?"

"No, there isn't," Brown said. "There's no connection. But Bromfield did talk to Hershon and you might learn something there." Brown turned back to the warden to see if there would be anything more to add, and plainly there was not.

Then Brown ushered Branden out into Anita Falviano's office and asked him to wait while he spoke with Warden Franks. When he emerged twenty minutes later, Brown was red in the face and angry.

"Hershon is the only way to go," he said, "and if you've got the time, we can do it now."

Branden gathered his jacket and stood by the door. Brown said, "Right, OK," lifted the receiver from Falviano's desk phone, and punched out four digits. He spoke several crisp sentences to the guards on duty at the prison and escorted Branden out of the offices and through red iron doors into the old fortress prison.

24

Monday, June 16
6:00 A.M.

TWO plumbers in coveralls walked into the sandstone courthouse in Millersburg that Monday morning with Bruce Robertson. By 6:45 A.M., the four urinals in the third-floor men's room
were lying on the floor, their service pipes capped off at the
wall. Next came two of the three toilets in the stalls, plus the
privacy dividers. As the plumbers wheeled the porcelain fixtures
to a janitor's closet down the hall, Amish carpenters arrived in
a long passenger van driven by one of Robertson's deputies.

Saturday, all of the supplies had been delivered according to
Robertson's orders. Two-by-fours, two-by-eights, brick, mortar, nails, wheelbarrows, sheets of bulletproof glass, and two
reinforced steel doors. Everything was now stacked in the hall
outside the men's room, adjacent to the courtroom of Judge
Harrold S. Singleton.

The carpenters came into the courthouse up the steep east
steps, carrying their wooden tool trays, saws, levels, and squares.
They were dressed nearly alike. Work boots, plain denim trousers, denim vests or light denim jackets, long-sleeved shirts that
varied in color, but were all uniformly plain. They wore light
yellow straw hats, and their hair stuck out, round and puffy
underneath. Some smoked. All left their lunch pails in the van.

On the third floor, the Amish crew looked over the men's
room, and milled about in the hall, as one older fellow, Gross-

vater to nearly all the men, checked in the adjoining court-room. He and Robertson spoke for a moment, and then the short, elderly Dutchman drew out a tape measure, walked off a length along a courtroom wall, and went out into the hall where the men lingered. He spoke for several minutes in Low German and slang, and soon the men began to busy themselves with their tools. They moved slowly, but purposefully. There was very little explanation for what anyone should do. They worked as a silent team that seemed to have done this sort of job a thousand times before. The labor was not rushed, nor were the minutes wasted.

A sledge was thrown against the wall in the men's room, and a rough doorway into the adjoining courtroom was knocked out. Ripping bars were taken to the trim work, and eventually the four walls in the men's room had been stripped back to the studs. One young fellow hammered together a couple of saw-horses, and two-by-eights were laid on top for a worktable. There was a great deal of measuring, writing, and cutting. There was occasional laughter, and sometimes good-natured teasing. By noon, the room was stripped bare, and the new doorway, from the old men's room into the courtroom, had been framed and squared. Then the heavy steel door was hinged and hung.

The Amish men ate their lunches on the east steps of the courthouse. Locals who passed by gave them little notice. Some tourists lingered and snapped photos. The occasional buggy was brought in and hitched at the rail near the sheriff's van.

During the break, Robertson walked over from the jail, stud-ied the progress on the third floor, and came out onto the east steps. The men sprawled casually on the stone steps, and some lay flat on their backs in the grass below. The one who first noticed Robertson said something in German slang, and the Grossvater pulled himself up from his lunch and climbed the steps to talk with the sheriff.

After lunch, the two youngest boys hauled water in buckets

from the second floor and mixed mortar with shovels in a wheelbarrow, while two others laid brick. Two men stacked brick for the masons, and two others worked in the courtroom to install a bulletproof panel in front of the steel door. By three o'clock, Robertson's brick room was finished, and deputies carried in a simple bed frame and mattress. When it was ready, they collected the sheriff from his office, and he looked the brick room over, while the Amish men watched.

Robertson started in the courtroom. There was a tall shield of bulletproof glass with a table and four chairs set behind the glass. Behind the chairs, on the south wall at the side of the courtroom, there was a black steel door. Robertson opened the door and stepped through, into the old men's room. All but one toilet had been removed, as well as all but one sink. The walls were entirely of new red brick, and even the one outside window had been bricked over. One of the four brick walls had a small window of bulletproof glass, and, behind a steel door in that wall, there was an anteroom where a deputy could watch a prisoner through the glass. The other door in the anteroom opened into the hallway on the third floor of the courthouse. The ceiling in the brick room was covered over with Plexiglas to put the electric fixtures out of reach to a prisoner. Robertson sat on the bed and weighed his procedures one last time.

He had ordered the bulletproof glass a week ago, after they had first learned about David Hawkins. The idea of the brick room had come to him in a single flash. The details had formed in his mind on a sleepless night. Now he sat where Sands would sit, and thought it over from every angle he could see. Sands would be brought over at night. He'd already approved the overtime and told the deputies. In the days to come, Sands would live in the sheriff's brick box for as long as his trial lasted. The heavy curtains on the courtroom windows would forestall a sniper's run at Sands during a trial, but there was now also the bulletproof partition as an extra security measure. The steel doors were more than adequate. The anteroom would allow them to watch Sands around the clock. The hot water had been turned off in the sink, and the bricks covered everything else that Sands might think to use as a weapon. When he was satisfied, Robertson walked out, settled up with the Amish boss, and strolled back to his office in the jail.

Sands was scheduled to go over Thursday night. Robertson rocked back in his chair and smoked. Sands would actually go over Monday night, tonight, and only Robertson knew it. Then Sands would sit out his trial in a brick cocoon, because, Robertson told himself with satisfaction, no U.S. Army Special Forces clown was going to get to Sands before his trial. Not on Robertson's watch. Not in Robertson's town. When the time came, he'd throw the switch on Sands himself. But until then, anyone who wanted Sands dead was going to have to blow the courthouse completely apart in order to do it.

25

Monday, June 16
4:20 P.M.

EVERYTHING about Billy Hershon spoke of malicious hostil-
ity. His voice, his words, his tone. His walk, his rock-and-sway,
street-gang swagger. His eyes. He stood on the prisoner's side
of the glass partition and seemed both scornful and amused.
Branden was seated on the outside. Lieutenant Brown stood
behind him. Branden lifted the receiver and held it to his ear.
He leaned back casually, propped an elbow on the armrest of
the chair, and gave a long, unconcerned sigh, all the while holding Hershon's gaze.

Hershon yanked the receiver off the wall on his side of the
glass and spoke disrespectfully. "The Man, there, says you've
got something for me on Jesse."

"I've got a lot for you on Jesse Sands," Branden replied with
a disinterested nonchalance. Brown stood back and observed
the exchange. "Hold back as much as you can," he had told the
professor. "Trade every fact for another one like it. Never tell
everything and surely nothing that isn't returned in kind. And
never allow yourself to appear concerned." So far, Branden had
performed well.

"Where is he?" Hershon asked.

"In Ohio. Tell me about him."

"Where in Ohio?" His eyes were dead with spite.

"Tell me about him."

Hershon rattled off Sands's prison number and said, "Maxed out," followed by an intense, "WHERE IN OHIO?"

"Millersburg. Tell me why . . ."

"How do you know him?" Hershon took a seat.

"I've spoken to him once."

"He's back in?" Disappointment appeared on Hershon's face for the briefest of moments.

"County jail. Now tell me why you're not surprised."

"Because he was gonna push." His expression changed from disappointment to satisfied anticipation.

"Push what?"

"Push The Man, fool. What'd he do?"

"You tell me."

Hershon slammed the flat palm of his free hand against the partition and curled his fingers as if he were clawing through the reinforced glass. "What'd Jesse do?"

Branden stared back, fought an internal battle with his nerves, hung up the receiver slowly, stood, and turned to walk out.

Hershon shouted a profusion of curses into the phone, and Branden turned back to face him. Slowly and deliberately, he came back to the phone, lifted the receiver, and stood in place behind the glass, listening.

Hershon barked, "What?"

"I asked you a question," Branden said with as much insolence as he could muster.

"He offed The Man, didn't he."

"I wouldn't know. He killed a young girl," Branden said. He let the futility of the conversation show on his face as boredom.

Hershon broke into a cautious smile.

Branden stood with the receiver to his ear and waited with an uninformative expression. "Tell me about Jesse Sands," Branden said.

"I told him how to get The Man."

"Which means?"

"You figure it out. Aren't you supposed to be some kind of professor?"

"Why would you have told Sands to have done anything?"

"Who's got him locked up?" Hershon asked. Branden realized the question wasn't a change of topic.

"Holmes County Sheriff. Why'd you tell Sands something like that?"

"Told Jesse lots of things in eight years sleeping together."

"Why's he so unconcerned to be locked away for murder?"

"If it weren't that, it'd be something else, sooner or later."

"That's rather fatalistic, wouldn't you say?"

"Cut the crap, Professor. Where's Millersburg?"

"Like I said, Ohio."

"County jail?"

"Right. Now tell me about Jesse Sands."

"He did the max, here. Now he's back inside, somewhere else. What'd you expect?"

"You say that as if it were of no consequence."

"It isn't. Now tell me what happened."

"He killed a girl."

Hershon drew closer to the glass. "Tell me about that."

"Why was Sands in prison?" Branden asked.

"He raped some bitch. How'd he kill her?"

"Shot her. Raped who?"

"Some old lady, twenty years ago. Shot her where?"

"In the chest. What'd you mean he did the max?"

"No parole. Not where, *where*? He shot her where?"

"In her own home. He took the maximum sentence?"

"Do the whole stretch and you're free. Daytime or night?"

"What do you mean?"

"Did he kill her at night or in the day?"

"Night. What did Sands talk about when he was in?"

"How'd he get caught?"

"What did he talk about?"

"How'd he get caught?"

Branden waited purposefully.

"Revenge."

"Meaning?"

"Sands talked about revenge. How'd he get caught?"

"The police grabbed him outside the girl's house with the gun he used to shoot her. Revenge for what?"

"Tell me exactly how he was caught."

Branden gave it to him in detail and asked, "Revenge for what?"

But Billy Hershon never answered. He thought for a moment longer about the story Branden had told him of Jesse Sands's capture. His eyes narrowed at one point and then opened again. A distant look appeared in his gaze, and then he refocused his cold eyes on the professor. In his expression, there was the unmistakable pride of a grand triumph. Jesse Sands's triumph. A satisfied smile, a victorious swagger, and Hershon disappeared behind the door into the cellblocks.

26

Monday, June 16
4:45 P.M.

"YOU said William Erlanger called you himself?" Cal asked from the passenger seat of Caroline Branden's car.

Caroline drove east on Route 39 and said, "Yes. He said David Hawkins had been out to his long-distance rifle range yesterday."

"Did he say he saw David?" Cal asked.

"I'm not sure, Cal. We've just got this appointment this afternoon. That's about all I know. Erlanger said it couldn't wait for Michael to come home from New Jersey."

"Have you heard from Mike?"

"Just a brief call before I came to pick you up. It was all a dead end in New Jersey."

After turning onto a small township road, they soon saw the Erlanger rifle range on old farmland. They found the almost unnoticeable little sign beside the road, pulled into the gravel lane, and drove over a rise, around two sharp corners, and onto the gravel lot behind the firing line. Cars, trailers, and campers were aligned in rows behind two concrete buildings, and several dozen people strolled among the campers and the buildings of the range.

In front of the white concrete buildings was the firing line, under a long roof of corrugated metal sheeting on high poles. Range officers in orange jackets patrolled both ends of the line, and a man in an orange vest sat in a wooden tower behind the line. Under the long roof, on benches made of double-thick concrete blocks, sat dozens of shooters. Most of them worked quietly beside their rifles, but occasionally, one would take a shot.

At the end of the current thirty-minute relay, the man in the tower spoke into a loudspeaker. "Cease fire!"

His ceasefire command was parroted at the ends of the firing line by the two range officers on foot. "Cease fire; cease fire."

"Open all actions!"

"Open all actions; open all actions." Actions clicked open, up and down the line.

"Empty all chambers!"

"Empty all chambers; empty all chambers." Chambers emptied out, everywhere along the line.

"Bench all firearms!"

"Bench all firearms; bench all firearms." From one end of the line to the other, men and women secured a firm purchase on their ornate rifles, and lifted them into vertical positions in wooden racks.

"Stand clear of all firearms and make the line safe!"

"Stand clear of all firearms and make the line safe; stand clear of all firearms and make the line safe." Up and down the line, men and women stepped back from their rifles.

Now the range officers moved from their positions at either end of the firing line to inspect each shooter and each rifle. The officer on the right reported first to the tower. "Line is clear on the right!"

A similar announcement soon came from the officer on the left. "Line is clear on the left!"

The man in the tower announced: "The range is closed. You will have one-half hour to post and pull targets."

"The range is closed; the range is closed."

For the first time since Caroline and Cal had arrived, the shooters moved about casually on the firing line and behind it.

Before, they had seemed controlled, deliberate, absorbed with their shots. Now, most of the shooters were milling about, talking, or were taking a fresh target downrange, at two hundred yards.

As they stood there, the range officer from the tower arrived with a telescope mounted on a tripod. He was a big man, soft-spoken and gentle, but given a megaphone, the absolute master of authority on the line. "I'm Erlanger. I presume you must be Caroline Branden." He set the tripod and telescope on the lawn in front of them.

Caroline answered "Yes" as Erlanger sighted-in the telescope and focused on the distant targets.

"I take it that neither of you has been to a benchrest target range before. Have a look."

He stepped back from the telescope and took a position behind them. They each took a turn at the eyepiece. At the end of the two hundred yards, there were small squares of paper with thin grid lines in black. At the center of the targets, there was a small bull's-eye.

It was Caroline who asked the obvious question, while peering through the scope. "How big are the targets?"

She lifted her head from the scope, and turned to hear Erlanger's answer. He had anticipated the question and stood silently displaying a sample, and a satisfied smile. The target was no bigger than a half-piece of typing paper, and the precise grid lines inscribed a black circle no larger than a quarter. As Cal inspected the target more closely, Caroline returned to the telescope.

"I can't see any hits, Mr. Erlanger. Why are they taking down targets that have no bull's-eyes?"

"Look off-center, about an inch or two from the bull's-eye," Erlanger answered.

"Oh, I see. Yes. Little bullet holes," and then the next obvious question, "Why doesn't anyone seem to be able to hit the bull's-eye?"

Erlanger said, "I can help you with that question," and asked them to follow him on a tour. They stepped away from the firing line, and followed him into the stand of trailers that were parked on the grounds.

As Erlanger led them among the trailers, he pointed out some of the license plates and said, "We get shooters from all over the world here." There were dozens of license plates from other states, and insignias on trailers from other countries. Germany, South Africa, Australia, Finland, and Switzerland.

Erlanger led them into one of the clubhouses. "We've been a worldwide center for benchrest competitions for ten or twelve years now. We hold them every summer, right here in Ohio." In the clubhouse, there were trophies and displays, as well as magazines, supplies, concessions, equipment, and shooting gear for sale.

Cal stepped up to a glass case and studied the inscriptions on the trophies. Most of them bore Erlanger's name, from matches in the United States and abroad. Cal noted trophies from France, Finland, Austria.

Next, Erlanger led them into an adjacent building where several rifles were in various stages of manufacture in the first two rooms. "The reason we're known for benchrest competitions is because of our rifles. We make what I consider to be the finest, most accurate benchrest rifle in the world. We use Hart barrels from New York, made of stainless steel, and we tune their lengths like the pipes of an organ. The actions are machined to such precise tolerances that we need computerized technology to cut them out." He pointed to giant, automated lathes and drills, Mazak CNC machines that effortlessly and methodically carved complicated rifle actions out of aluminum blocks.

In another room, Erlanger showed them five or six massive

green machine tools where three men worked to polish and finish the actions. Bolts lay around the room on shelves, in line for assembly, polished and finished to a supreme brightness. "We use certain parts from Remington firing pin assemblies, but refinish each bolt in six separate hand steps. Some of these lathes helped to win World War II, and now they turn out the most accurate rifle components in the world. Poetic, don't you think? The barrels are fluted to conserve weight, and they're glass bedded and free floated in polymer stocks. We use 7075 aircraft aluminum in the actions and for the scope rings. That conserves weight too, but requires a perfect fit on the bearing surfaces. There aren't many outfits in the world that can duplicate our rifle."

Outside, Erlanger said, "I hope you'll be able to appreciate my point, Mr. Troyer. The reason I called you, Mrs. Branden. It's all a matter of precision. Our rifles have to be made to extremely precise tolerances. And every rifle we make is meant to be exactly like the others in one respect. They are the most accurate and precise rifle in the world at two hundred to three hundred yards."

"You made David Hawkins's rifle for him?" Caroline asked.

"Yes," Erlanger said. "I tried to talk him out of the blue sparkle polymer for the stock, though." He laughed in recollection. "Tacky, really. Fifties-style. But he said he'd had a steering wheel like that, on one of his first cars when he was a kid, and he wanted the rifle that way too. No trouble to oblige him. After he won the '89 match, we've gotten a lot of requests for the same color."

As they walked back to the firing line, Caroline said, "You still haven't told us why no one hits the bull's-eye."

Erlanger explained. "Benchrest shooting is a precision sport. The winner is the one who can put one round after another into precisely the same spot. The winner is the one who has the smallest hole in the target after five rounds have been logged, sometimes ten. It takes tremendous concentration and a lifetime of practice to be able to do that at two hundred yards. Benchrest shooters require the best rifles that can be made. They make their own ammunition, because factory ammo is not nearly reliable enough."

"But why not hit what you shoot at?" Caroline asked.

"Because in this sport, Mrs. Branden, you'd hit it," Erlanger said.

"I don't follow," Caroline said.

"The demands of benchrest shooting are relentless. Wind, weather, even barometric pressure can influence a shot. Sometimes shooters will bring their reloading equipment to the range just to be able to make up a slightly different load, in case the weather changes. Under those sorts of constraints, and at two hundred yards, a shooter doesn't want the shape or appearance of the bull's-eye to change with each shot that hits it."

"The shooter preserves the bull's-eye in order to have something better to aim at?" Caroline asked.

"Wouldn't you?" Erlanger said.

Cal eyed the big man nervously and asked, "You said on the phone that you've seen David Hawkins."

"I didn't see him, myself. Others say they saw him. But he was here all right, yesterday for about an hour. He left his targets posted when he had finished. Nobody in the world would pull down a David Hawkins target. If he doesn't come back, those targets'll stay posted until they fall down of their own accord."

Erlanger led them up to his spotting scope, and asked one of the line officers, "Is that Hawkins's target from yesterday?"

"Yes, sir, five shots as near as I remember."

"Right," Erlanger said. "Hawkins took his first five shots in half an hour at the range. That's way too fast for him."

"Did you notice the flags, George?" the range officer asked.

At fifty-yard intervals, reaching out toward David Hawkins's target, they saw several long, narrow, yellow silk flags, each attached, about two feet off the ground, to thin white poles. Each now registered the faintest cross-range breeze.

"Wind markers," Erlanger explained.

Next, Erlanger motioned to the eyepiece, and made way for Cal. "Mr. Troyer, I wonder if you'd be willing to tell me what you make of that target."

Cal stepped up to the spotting scope and peered downrange. He focused carefully, studied the target for a while, and then looked up from the eyepiece to Erlanger. "I know about these sighter targets from the service," Cal remarked.

Erlanger waited silently, and Cal returned to his observation. Then he spoke for the record. He called the shots in order of fire, as they lay on a standard NRA six-bull scope-zeroing target, left to right for the top row of three bull's-eyes, and again left to right for the bottom row of three.

"Five shots. Last bull blank because he didn't need it. First shot at 2 o'clock; an inch high and an inch and a half right of center."

"That's Hawkins's typical hit, judging from the target Michael and I saw at his house," Caroline said.

Cal lifted his eye from the scope and looked back at Erlanger for confirmation. Getting that, he returned to the eyepiece.

"A second shot at twelve o'clock, dead center but an inch high. Hawkins must have made a windage adjustment. Third, fourth, and fifth shots all dead-center bull's-eyes. An elevation adjustment. Now he's dead-on."

"And you conclude . . ?"

"He's sighted in his benchrest rifle on the bull's-eye."

"Correct."

"Let me see," Caroline said. When she looked up from the scope, Cal took another turn at the eyepiece and groaned.

Erlanger moved the scope out to focus at a greater distance, made a careful adjustment with the eyepiece and said, "That's not the end of it." He rechecked his spot and waved Troyer up to the eyepiece. The scope was focused on a thin slip of yellow silk, fluttering gently in the distance. Cal peered downrange, and Erlanger added, "That's David Hawkins's flag posted at three hundred yards."

Cal suffered an inner wave of numbing hopelessness, and put his hands on top of his head as if he had surrendered. Caroline looked again into the scope and realized that any lingering doubts that her husband might recently have held about David Hawkins would now transform themselves into a fatal resignation.

Caroline asked, "Is there another target out there?"

When Erlanger had repositioned the scope, they each peered downrange and saw another NRA scope adjustment target, with the same two rows of three bulls each. The first two bull's-eyes in the top row of three had bullet holes that had fallen low, the first more so than the last. The third was nearly on, and the last three bull's-eyes on the bottom row had six-millimeter holes, dead center on the bull's-eyes.

Erlanger let them adjust their thoughts to that vision, and then he said, "Now let me explain something about David Hawkins. David shoots a 6 mm PPC. He uses 68-grain Berger bullets made in Phoenix. I've heard him say that, with Hodgdon powder, he can push them out at over 3,500 feet per second. That's movin' out, in anybody's book. But the key to David's success has been attention to detail. As you've seen from his little yellow flags, he notes the wind downrange. He knows the atmospheric pressure on the day of a match. His 36-power scope is so powerful that he can see the grains in the paper target, even at three-hundred yards. And on hot days, he watches the heat shimmers in the scope. He notices the patterns that heat convection produces at the target when he takes his first shot. Then he waits for the identical shimmer pattern before he takes another shot. Precision. He never fails. Coolest trigger I've ever known. He knows how to calm his heartbeat, because with a

36-power scope, the pulse in your trigger finger will shake the scope as it holds on the target. He slows his heartbeat when he's about to fire a shot. And here's the thing. If his scope is sighted in on you, you're going to bleed. That's all there is to it."

In the car, on the drive back to Millersburg, Cal Troyer began to pray. When Caroline pulled the car up to the Raber farm, he seemed at first not to know where he was. When he recognized the farm and roused himself, he climbed out, walked up the lane to the big house, and turned inside without speaking. He had an utterly crestfallen and bewildered expression on his face, and, for the first time, his mind and heart seemed battered by cruel doubts, the temptation to lose faith in David Hawkins nearly overpowering him.

27

Monday, June 16
5:10 P.M.

FOLLOWING *them down the lane to the rifle range would have been a monstrously stupid mistake. He could see that now. But it had been close. Another near-fatal error. Too many, now. Too much on the line. He closed his eyes and relived the shattering, unbearable hours when Branden had gone to New Jersey. The risk to have let him go there unfollowed. To have let him go there at all. To even have let him live.*

Going back to check the bugs at the Brandens' had been worth the risk. The call Branden had made from Trenton had delivered him. Now it was clear that Branden had not figured out anything at all. Nothing. Perhaps he never would. At least not in time to matter.

No need to follow them, now. He had gotten it all when Erlanger had called Caroline. Fools. Sightless country fools. It'd all be over before any of them caught a clue.

Now, just wait it out. Follow them back into town, and watch for signs of trouble. If any of it started to unravel, he always had the .22 and the silencer. Do Branden out in the country. Lure him there with a phone call, and it'd be days before they found him. Even if they did, Sands would still go down for Janet Hawkins. And whatever else might happen, no matter the cost, he promised himself again that Sands was going to pay.

28

Monday, June 16
11:30 P.M.

HALF of the deputies and half of the Holmes County Sheriff's
Reserve found themselves called to duty at various stations near
the center of Millersburg. Bruce Robertson had them stationed
at precise locations near the courthouse. There were squad cars
to block traffic on each street leading to the courthouse, with
instructions to use no lights. Ellie Troyer was on the dispatch
radio, with instructions to call those cars into place when Robertson appeared in the front room with Jesse Sands. Six deputies
patrolled the sidewalks around the jail and the courthouse,
armed with 12-gauge pumps and their duty pistols. Two more
deputies would go with Robertson into the cells, each carrying
a shotgun. Ricky Niell followed Robertson in, carrying leg irons,
a waist restraint, and handcuffs. Robertson said, "Not the leg
irons, Ricky," and then all was ready.

Robertson, Niell, Wilsher, and Schrauzer pushed through the
iron door abruptly, rousted Sands from his sleep, threw him onto
the floor, bound his wrists to an iron band around his waist, and
stood him upright in his cell. Sands protested, and Robertson
yanked his head back by the top of his sandy hair.

"You're gonna walk, Sands, and you're not gonna say a
word," Robertson snapped.

As they pulled Sands toward the cell door, he shouted and
tried to twist free of the deputies. Robertson swung his night-

stick against the back of Sands's legs, dropping him forward on his knees.

Robertson said, "Gag him," and Ricky Niell produced a wad of cloth and a leather strap. He pushed the cloth into Sands's mouth, wrapped the strap around to the back of his head, and tied it off with force. Then Niell jerked Sands to his feet and pushed him through the door. When Ellie saw them coming down the steps at the far end of her hall, she called for the cars to block the streets, and when they were in place, Robertson nodded. "We're going in the side door. Right?" he said.

The deputies nodded grimly, and Robertson led the way out the front door of the jail. It took less than fifteen seconds for them to run Sands into the side entrance of the darkened court-house. Without stopping, they ran him up the long steps from the basement, and then up the two long stairways to the third floor. Their feet pounded out a furious commotion on the old wooden floors as they pushed ahead in the dark. On the third floor, they ran to the remodeled men's room, pushed Sands through the door into Robertson's custom brick room, dropped him onto the single cot, and untied his gag.

Sands squirmed and fought against his cuffs and tried to struggle to his feet in the dark. Robertson sent one deputy back to give Ellie the word, and he put two deputies on the door. When Ellie got the go-ahead, she called in the squad cars, and the deputies out on the lawn poured into the darkened courthouse and took up positions that Robertson had earlier designated. By the end of the operation, Jesse Sands found himself in a brick-lined room, with a cot, a toilet, and a cold-water sink.

When a deputy hit the light switch in the outside observation room, Sands looked around and growled, "This is a stinking toilet."

"That's right, Sands, it's your own special little stinking toilet," Robertson sneered.

There were four men in the outer room, and Niell inside

with Robertson and Sands. Robertson eyed Sands with contempt, and looked around at his handiwork with a satisfied expression. The deputies waited.

Sands rose off his cot and moved threateningly toward the sheriff. Robertson caught him across the face with his nightstick and dropped him to the floor. Then Robertson pushed a knee into Sands's back and ordered the deputies to unlock the restraints on his waist and wrists. When Robertson let Sands up, he sat on the edge of his cot and rubbed at his wrists.

"This is your new home, Sands," Robertson said. "You're going to trial through that door, and you're gonna live inside a brick box until we're done with you here."

"You country slobs won't convict me of anything," Sands snarled. "I've got lawyers."

Robertson said, "Niell, I want you to take my sidearm and my nightstick and back out of here. Close the door and don't open it until I tell you to."

Niell obeyed.

Sands relaxed and lay back on the small bed. Robertson waited until the steel door was closed, and then he yanked Sands up by the shoulders and jammed his back against the brick wall inside Sands's new cell. The palms of both the sheriff's massive hands were planted flat on either side of Sands's neck. Robertson's jaw was set like a cocked hammer, eyes blazing heat, a snarl on his lips.

Sands started to say something, but Robertson drew back his fist, and Sands swallowed his words. Robertson forced himself close enough that he could have clipped eyelashes off Sands's face with his teeth.

"Shut up, Sands," he growled, taking hold of Sands's throat. "Shut up or I'll stomp a hole in you right here. I don't care a rat's hole, as you can plainly see, whether or not you draw another breath. But I do care about my good name, so you're not checking out on my watch. After your trial, I'll stand in line to light you up. But if you have to sleep in a brick toilet for a month in order to save my good name, then that's what you're gonna do."

The sheriff eased his grip on Sands's throat. "You're not gonna die in my custody, Sands, that's just the way it is. But here's a little something for you. One day down the road, not right away, because your lawyer will appeal, but someday you're gonna fry for Janet Hawkins. You're gonna sit down on that old wooden frame of a chair, and I'll be there. The governor of this fine state owes me a favor or two, and I'll be there to throw the switch on you, myself.

"Oh, sure, guys like Cal Troyer will try to save your soul. But that day, Sands, it'll be just you and me, and I'll be the one who's smiling. I'm gonna drop-kick your worthless hide into the next world, and it won't be too cruel. Won't be too unusual. It won't be even a little bit sad. That day'll come, Sands, soon enough, and I'm gonna send you back to your maker.

"You see, Sands, Cal Troyer and his type believe in a God of love, mercy, and forgiveness. Well, that may be true, but I don't get too worked up on that particular angle. Makes sense, you see, but I just don't get emotional about it like Troyer does. No, Sands, I take it a step further. I see a God of justice. Justice for people like Janet Hawkins. And justice for scum like you."

29

Tuesday, June 17
10:00 A.M., and later that night

CAROLINE met the professor at the baggage claim, lower level, of Cleveland Hopkins International Airport. She had driven their small truck, and he tossed his one bag into the truck bed and climbed in on the passenger's side. As she drove, he recounted for her the fruitless hours he had spent in New Jersey.

In turn, she told of the afternoon she and Cal had spent at Erlanger's rifle range. When she described how Hawkins had zeroed his scope, the professor urged her to retell it with all the details.

"The first targets were posted at two hundred yards," she said. "Each shot he took brought him closer to zero. The last shot was dead on.

"Erlanger showed us Hawkins's little yellow flags on white poles. Windage markers. He said Hawkins can see heat shimmers in his scope, and that he slows his pulse for a shot. Then Erlanger moved his telescope to focus on other targets, at more than three hundred yards. More little flags there, too. The first shots in this second set were low, and the last one was a dead-center bull's-eye."

Branden thought of Jesse Sands and fell silent as Caroline drove south on I-71. "Michael," Caroline said at last. "Have you ever been to Hawkins's house at night, like when Janet Hawkins was killed?"

"No," Branden said, rousing with her question.

"Do you know everything that happened that night between Sands and Greyson?"

"No," Branden complained.

"I'll go over there tonight," he said. "Try to see what it was like when Greyson captured Sands."

By nightfall, a breeze from the north had stiffened, and the temperature had dropped twenty degrees. A cool mist gave way to a drizzle, and then a soaking downpour. By 10:00 P.M., the professor was standing in the rain, wearing a long, black, hooded poncho, in front of a neighborhood bar on the west end of town.

The Budweiser sign out by the street was shining. There were two cars in the gravel lot beside the old green house. He climbed the wooden steps onto the porch and entered through the steel door with a small diamond of heavy glass for a window. Two old cigarette machines stood inside the door. Two of the booths held customers.

The bartender was a short man with tattoos. He dried his hands on a white apron that hung at his waist and drew Branden a beer. He said he remembered Sands. Branden nursed the beer, not liking it especially, and asked about the night when Jesse Sands had sat on the last barstool, drinking alone.

Leaving his beer half finished, Branden paid up, went out through the back door, and found himself near the intersection of two alleys in the old neighborhoods of Millersburg. He checked his location against his memory of where the Hawkins house stood, and started off in that direction.

In ten minutes he had found the right house from the alley in back. The key in his pocket let him in through the door on the back porch. He felt his way in the dark as Sands must have done. From memory, he found the kitchen and then the door that let out onto the side door landing.

He turned in the dark to the swinging door on his right and

pushed through into the dining room. He felt his way into the living room and found the steps to the second floor. He sat on the steps thinking about Jesse Sands for a while, about his movements the night he shot Janet Hawkins. Slowly, his eyes adjusted to the dim street light coming through the front windows. He worked his way back to the kitchen, where he went through the door to the basement stairs.

On the landing, he felt for the wall switch to the basement lights, but out of a vague sense of familiarity, he did not throw the switch. Instead, Branden felt his way down the steps in the dark.

Again, there was the background hum of dehumidifiers in the basement. The faint oiled aroma of the machine tools. The wooden block was in its secret place under the stairs. The hidden toggle switch once again activated the electric bolts to the hidden door in the wall behind him. The door turned inward noiselessly when he pushed. He closed the door behind himself, took five paces across the darkened room, found the padded stool, and sat down, unnerved to the point of distraction to have understood the power and resolve that David Hawkins surely now possessed, as he made his plans with his newly zeroed rifle.

Branden remembered Cal Troyer, out at the Raber farm, and then Abigail, her outward beauty marred by a single scar, her inward beauty measureless. He thought of Herman P. Raber's great-grandfather and the homestead cabin where Abigail and Hawkins were to have been married. He thought of Nancy Blain, and Eric Bromfield. He thought of Marty Holcombe, preparing to run as much of the stories as Bromfield had managed to finish before he was killed. He thought of Bruce Robertson's limitless, manic determination to guard Jesse Sands. He thought of Ricky Niell, not at all convinced that the sheriff was actually right about David Hawkins. He thought of Brown, the chief security officer for Warden Franks, uncomfortable with the way the warden had handled matters in New Jersey. Of Billy Hershon's smoldering animosity and his cold celebration of hate. And Nabal Greyson in a dilapidated walk-up apartment in Millersburg, overlooking the courthouse and the jail next door.

Then there was Sands. What motivated him? What had Sands meant by what he told David Hawkins in the jail that night, precipitating the defining crisis of Hawkins's present and future life? Finally, there was David Hawkins, himself. Since his night with Cal Troyer at the jail, David Hawkins had . . . What? As far as Branden knew, Hawkins had actually done only two things. He had made up a batch of high-performance ammo, and he had sighted-in his rifle at three hundred-odd yards, using yellow windage markers. And why do that if not to kill Jesse Sands?

But Hawkins had an alternative. He was to inherit, with Abigail, the best of the precious farmland that Holmes County had to offer. He'd have a lifetime of safety and peace to enjoy. His immediate family would extend to dozens of households, every Brother and Sister ready to help at a moment's notice. He'd have a life so far removed from the government and greater America that soon his nightmares of combat would fade, and he'd end his days peacefully in his own bed, grandchildren near his side. David Hawkins had more to lose than any of them did. So why the rifle?

Branden closed his eyes as he sat in the dark. The black poncho rustled when he moved, and drizzled water onto the concrete floor of the private armory room. He turned the jagged forms of the puzzle over in his mind and saw nothing new in any of them. Still the press of rolling time seemed almost palpable to him. Tomorrow, Nabal Greyson would stand on the courthouse steps and accept a citation from the mayor. Two days later, Jesse Sands would find himself in the courtroom of Judge Harrold S. Singleton. By this time next month, Sands would likely have been transferred to Lucasville State Prison. And by then, the fate of David Hawkins and Abigail Raber would have been crystallized for eternity, like a diamond. Or would it be graphite? Abigail and David still stood a chance of coming through this affair with their future together intact. If only Hawkins would forsake revenge.

But that all depended on the actions of Hawkins alone. David Hawkins himself would determine his path into the future. By this time next week, he'd either have moved into the cabin with Abigail at the back of the Raber fields, or he'd have moved himself out of state, beyond the reach of Bruce Robertson. He'd either have walked away, free, into the life of peace, or he'd have run away, with the burden of vengeance crushing him.

Then, abruptly, as he sat in the dark on the tall stool next to David Hawkins's loading bench in the secret back basement armory, Branden caught the unmistakable aroma of a pungent cigar. He slipped quietly off the stool, eased across the floor, opened the secret door, and saw the red-glowing end of Nabal Greyson's cigar in the dark, blocking his way up the steps.

Greyson leaned back against the far wall in the dark, knocked ash off his cigar, and said, in his graveled voice, with a self-congratulating tone, simply, "Professor."

30

NABAL Greyson stood in the dark at the bottom of the basement steps and drew purposefully on his cigar. Branden could
hear him there, shaking rainwater off his jacket, and he could
see the glowing cigar. The first pulses of adrenaline began to
subside in Branden as he stood his position next to the step risers. He focused his eyes on the red tip of the cigar and quietly
lifted his hand to the toggle switch. The electric bolts slid home
with their faint, nearly inaudible whir. He replaced the wooden
block and moved right, toward the machine tools. He found
the tall green metal drill press, fumbled for the switch on its
small spotlight, and turned it on in time to see Greyson moving
toward him, caught offguard by the shaft of intense light, jerk-
ing his right arm behind his back to hide the heavy object in his
hand. Branden pulled the adjustable light from its position over
the drill press's flat metal stage and aimed it at Greyson's face.

Nabal Greyson's wet gray hair lay flat against his scalp,
slicked back straight from his forehead. He caught his cigar between his teeth and ran the palm of his left hand across each
eyebrow and back over his forehead to clear rainwater from his
eyes. His right arm stayed locked in place behind his back.

Branden's mind took him in a dozen troublesome directions,
and his instincts cautioned him to flee.

"Why, Professor," Greyson said. "You surprise me. We've got

Sands in jail on a simple case of breaking and entering with murder, and you just can't seem to leave it alone."

Branden crossed to the lathe and snapped on its small light.
"Sorry, Greyson," he said. "Academic curiosity." He circled
around to the right and put the jigsaw between him and the
pallid Greyson.

Branden saw Greyson's right arm move forward an inch at
the shoulder and then halt. He watched Greyson's rheumy eyes
and realized Greyson was making a decision. The light jacket
that Greyson wore was thoroughly soaked by the rain. It clung
tightly to Greyson's ribs and betrayed a noticeable bulge under
his left arm. In the fraction of a second that it took the professor to understand what Greyson was doing, and as Greyson's
right arm started out from behind his back, Cal Troyer came
onto the landing above, caught the switch to the basement lights,
and called out, "Mike?" from the top of the steps. As Cal descended to the basement, Greyson reversed his arm abruptly,
fumbled for a moment at his beltline behind his back, turning
to put his back against a wall, brought his right hand around
empty, and calmly struck a match to relight his cigar.

Cal seemed surprised to find Greyson. To the professor he
said, "Mike," and nodded a cautious greeting. To Greyson he
said, "I'm Cal Troyer."

Greyson shifted his cigar to his left hand, stuck the thumb of
his right hand casually into his belt in front, and said, "Nabal
Greyson."

Troyer looked back and forth between Branden and Greyson,
then said to Branden, "Caroline told me I'd find you here."

Branden crossed between the machine tools to join Cal at
the bottom of the steps, and, because he couldn't think of anything else to say, he asked, "Any news of Hawkins?"

Cal nodded his head and said, "It's all taken care of, neat as
a pin. That's what I came over here to tell you."

Branden watched Greyson's eyes, and without looking at Cal, he asked, "You know something about David Hawkins?"

Greyson leaned back against the concrete basement wall and assumed a studiously casual pose.

Cal said, "There's a barn raising scheduled for next month out by a little cabin I know at the edge of a certain field. And I've had a long talk with a young woman who's to live there with her new husband. I've just come from their wedding."

Branden looked with surprise at Cal and asked, "They're married?"

Cal proudly asserted, "They could hold the Jesse Sands trial out on the courthouse lawn if they wanted to, and expect no harm from David Hawkins, Amish husband of the Raber line."

Greyson pushed off the wall, drew on his cigar with a strange, satisfied smirk, and stepped toward Cal, away from Branden. He eased the shoulder holster under his wet jacket into a more comfortable position, pulled the bottom seam of his jacket down in back to cover the silenced .22 stuck under his belt, and said, "That's all I've ever wanted." Then he climbed the basement stairs, and disappeared through the side door into the rain.

31

Wednesday, June 18
5:30 A.M.

CAROLINE Branden rose up from her pillow. She threw off the single sheet, tucked a few wayward strands of auburn hair behind her ears, and nudged the professor in the ribs. "Michael." She rustled him again. "How did he know it was you?"

Branden stirred, muttered something sleepily, and dropped back off. "Michael, how did Greyson know it was you in the basement?" He stirred again and came awake.

"How did he know it was you?" Caroline asked. "You said you had the lights out."

Branden opened his eyes and lay staring up at the ceiling. He cleared dreams from his mind and tried to think. Greyson had said, "Professor." That had been in the dark. In the basement. Half an hour after the professor had gone through the Hawkins's back door. Then Cal had arrived with news of the marriage of David Hawkins to Abigail Raber. He had thought it briefly strange that the marriage hadn't been held on the more traditional Thursday. But he hadn't found it strange to have imagined David Hawkins coming to Abigail and Cal. Making his peace with life. Taking his bride to the cabin by the woods.

But now he did have trouble with Caroline's simplest of questions. How had Greyson known? How had Greyson found him there in the dark? How had Greyson known who was there?

"I don't know," he said, and sat up.

"You had the lights out?" she asked.

"Yes."

"You'd been there for half an hour?"

"Maybe more."

"So, how'd he know it was you?"

He slid his legs over the edge of their bed, pulled the long green curtains back, and saw the first rays of light dawning in the east. He wandered into the bathroom, washed his face, combed his wavy hair, and brushed his short beard into place, thinking. Caroline went down to the kitchen and made a pot of coffee. On the long back porch, they watched the sun rise, and they talked.

"Where did you park?" Caroline asked.

"At the bar. Maybe five blocks away."

"How did you get to the Hawkins place?"

"Hiked in the rain, through the alleys."

"You said you went in through the back door. Maybe you turned the lights on."

"I didn't," Branden said, and then the obvious answer to Caroline's simple question tore through him like a thresher. "He must have followed me there."

A chill went through Caroline, and she shuddered. "Why?" she asked, obviously troubled.

Branden thought of Greyson in the dark outside the neighborhood bar where Sands had taken his drinks before he had murdered Janet Hawkins. It was the same bar where Branden, last night, had followed in Sands's path. He thought of his walk in the rain through the back alleys, and he realized that Greyson must have been there, close behind. He thought of Greyson watching him go in, and then of Greyson standing on the lawn in the backyard, waiting while Branden sat thinking in the dark, in Hawkins's back basement room.

"Greyson followed me there. Maybe starting at the bar. Maybe even earlier."

Caroline shivered and repeated, "But why?"

A good question, and the professor didn't know the answer. He frowned. "I'm going down to the courthouse for the mayor's ceremony," he said.

The doorbell rang, and Caroline answered it to find Branden's private secretary, Lawrence Mallory, at the door with a fax that had come in overnight at the college. Mallory gave her the fax, left, and Caroline began reading the letter as she came back down the front hall.

"Michael!" she exclaimed and hurried with the fax onto the back porch.

Branden rapidly scanned the bold scrawl on the first page.

> I can't let it go, Professor. The warden and your Mr. Greyson put in a few years together with the FBI when they were first getting started. They each had maybe ten years with the bureau. Greyson quit to take a job as a security officer at an Atlantic City casino. The attached article should tell you what you need to know. I think this is what got your reporter killed. Lt. Brown.

The second page was a fuzzy copy of an old newspaper article. Two pictures headlined side by side atop the article. The photo on the left was a mug shot of a young, angry-looking man, and the copy read: "Jesse Sands, convicted of rape and felonious assault." On the right, there was the unmistakable image of a young Nabal Greyson. The caption read: "Nabal Greyson, ex-FBI."

Branden muttered "Good grief," and read the story aloud.

> Ex-FBI agent Nabal Greyson has vowed that Jesse Sands, convicted of raping Greyson's fiancée Hazel Johnson in January of 1972, will never be granted early parole. "I will do everything I can to keep that monster in jail," Greyson said.
>
> The victim remains in an institution in Baltimore.

Greyson quit the FBI to remain near her. When asked
about Greyson's leaving the bureau, his former partner, FBI agent Allen Franks, said, "They were transfer-
ring us to Washington state. Nabal wanted to be on
hand whenever Sands comes up for parole."
The victim's condition has not improved, hospital
officials said. Greyson now works in Atlantic City as a
security guard.

Caroline fell into a wicker chair, stunned. Branden paced in
front of her, thinking, the pages of the fax hanging loose in his
fingers. "I'm going down to the courthouse," he said. "Please
try to phone Bruce to tell him what we've learned."

Branden dressed quickly and came back downstairs. Caroline
said, "They're all outside at the courthouse, Ellie says."

"I'm going down," Branden said. "Try Ellie again. Maybe she
can get word to Ricky Niell."

Branden came down off the college hills breaking the speed
limit. He jerked to a stop in the No Parking zone behind the jail,
and jogged around to the front of the jail on the courthouse
lawn.

Nancy Blain was there in jeans and a college T-shirt, two
cameras hanging from straps around her neck. As Branden came
onto the lawn near the big courthouse steps, she cranked off
several frames of the microphone stand, with the mayor and city
council president waiting next to Greyson at the top of the steps.
Marty Holcombe stood at the bottom of the steps with his arms
folded over his chest. Branden spotted Robertson on the lawn,
in full uniform. Out of the corner of his eye, Branden caught a
brief flutter of yellow.

It was a still, warm morning, skies hazy. The sandstone walls
and ornate windows of the courthouse seemed to hold a memory of the night air, cooling the heat of what promised to be a
sultry day. The sky gave only a hint of blue. It wasn't actually
cloudy, just the typical hazy gray, with its usual surplus of

humidity from the great lake to the north. The dull green copper roof of the courthouse seemed muted against the colorless sky. The traffic on the square had not yet built to its crescendo of tourist buses and Amish buggies. There were no buggies hitched at the rail.

On the top steps to the courthouse, a tall Amish carpenter carried his wooden tray of tools to the microphone and affixed a small round plaque to the microphone stand. The plaque carried the Millersburg City insignia. It was round, six inches in diameter, with a serrated edge painted gold. An ornate scroll ran across its center, bearing the Sheriff's Department motto— "To Serve and Protect."

The Amish carpenter left quietly, practically unobserved. The mayor motioned for Robertson, and the big sheriff came slowly off the lawn and up the steps. The four men posed there as Nancy Blain took photographs. Several more people assembled on the lawn and waited. The minutes passed.

Branden stood back from the crowd next to Ricky Niell and tugged nervously at his short brown beard. Again, his eye caught a flutter of yellow, and he stepped suddenly forward, walked left, and saw a small flag of yellow silk attached to a thin, white fiberglass pole, hooked into the top branches of a dogwood next to the courthouse steps. In a shattering instant, he realized what it meant.

The mayor stepped to the microphone and began his speech. Branden pulled Niell aside and rushed through an explanation about the yellow wind-marker flag in the branches of the dogwood. The city council president made his way to the microphone and began to speak. Branden and Niell separated on the lawn, searching for another yellow flag. At the back of the lawn, at the far corner near the intersection of Jackson and Clay, high atop a streetlight, Branden found the second fluttering strip of silk. Now, on the top step, Greyson moved to the podium and stood behind the microphone. Branden drew a line in his mind, connected the two yellow flags, and scanned the rooftops in the distance. Two hundred yards. Three hundred yards and there he saw a moment's flash of stainless steel and blue sparkle polymer on a rooftop, four long blocks away.

Branden shouted at Niell and tore for the courthouse steps. Niell fell in behind him, and Blain caught sight of them as they ran. Greyson's rasping voice came out strong on the loudspeakers, and Branden saw the whole tragedy play itself out in his mind. He understood in one frantic instant the meaning of what Jesse Sands had told David Hawkins that night at the jail. He saw Greyson in his mind, the night Janet Hawkins was murdered. Greyson, who must have followed Sands there in the rain. The unspeakable image of Greyson, waiting in the shadows that night as Sands broke into the house. Greyson in the dark, watching as Janet Hawkins walked unknowingly to her death. Greyson who first "arrived" after the gunshots, to drop Jesse Sands as he fled. Greyson who let Janet Hawkins die in order to put Sands down hard on a charge of murder. And, as he ran for the steps of the Millersburg courthouse, Branden understood why Jesse Sands had never been the target of David Hawkins. Understood that it was Greyson's unforgivable betrayal of his daughter that had drawn Hawkins here this morning with his rifle. He understood the detestable trap of vengeance that Greyson had laid for Jesse Sands, with Janet Hawkins as the bait. Janet Hawkins, murdered as much by Nabal Greyson's waiting in the dark as by the man who had actually pulled the trigger. And, as he ran for the steps, Professor Branden saw David Hawkins in his mind's eye, on a rooftop, four blocks away. He imagined the heat shimmers in Hawkins's scope. His finger tightening on the custom trigger. His pulse dropping to an undetectable whisper in his ears. His rifle balanced unwaveringly on a sandbag, the cross hairs settling onto Greyson's face.

Branden shouted, "Down!" and tore up the stone steps. The square receded into a vast, quiet space. His pounding footsteps registered on the stone in slow motion. Traffic noises disappeared. Greyson's crackling voice faded on the loudspeaker. The crowd turned to look. A camera on motor drive clicked and whirred in his right ear. Blain shouted as he passed her, but kept snapping shots. The men at the top of the steps backed up instinctively as they saw him approach. Greyson stood motionless behind the microphone, his right hand tucked under his left lapel.

Branden realized he was shouting. He heard the camera behind him on the steps, its metallic shutter snapping relentlessly. His momentum carried him forward. On the last step he threw himself forward, heard the shattering impact of an explosion, and saw the round plaque on the microphone stand disintegrate in front of Greyson's chest. He smashed into Greyson and knocked him over backwards against the sandstone walls. He expected another shot. It never came.

Greyson scrambled out from under Branden, jerked the professor fiercely to his feet by the neck, and slammed him against a sandstone pillar, infuriated. The professor opened his eyes and tried to focus on Greyson's apoplectic face.

With his left hand clutching the collar at Branden's throat, Greyson pushed the cold end of a .45 automatic into Branden's face. Greyson shouted something unintelligible to Branden, and then he reached up with his right thumb and cocked the hammer. There was a malicious sneer on his lips and a trace of spittle on his chin. A camera near at hand motored through frame after frame.

Greyson jerked ferociously on Branden's collar and lifted him from his feet. The top edge of the stone steps caught Greyson off balance, and he stumbled backwards. They toppled together down the steps, the .45 still fixed in Branden's face. Something shattered in Branden's leg.

The professor could see people around him shouting and

running, but he heard only the click and whir of Nancy Blain's Nikon. Ricky Niell came into view with his pistol drawn.

Greyson abruptly stopped shouting. He noticed the camera, and his grip on Branden's throat relaxed. Branden collapsed onto the steps of the courthouse, with his leg buckled underneath him, and with Greyson pulled down upon him. A wave of nausea engulfed Branden and then an unendurable, grinding pain. When he passed out, he was watching Ricky Niell and Bruce Robertson wrestle furiously with Greyson, to pull him up from the professor's shattered leg.

32

Thursday, June 19
5:45 P.M.

"PUSH the red button, Professor." The nurse put the gray metal box into his hand. He pushed. Slowly, the narcotic carried him back into the painless and lonely world of Morpheus, where strange faces hovered before him without personalities. Where empty rooms of pastel lights awaited him at the end of deserted hallways. Where blankness held him adrift in a whirling nightmare of weakness. He saw pastel worms lurching, hanging from the ceiling by the score. Great entangled monsters of metal and flesh hovering over him. Unending flashes of colors and forms of indecipherable shapes projected onto the inside of his eyelids.

There was a sip of ice water, and a moment's awareness of his leg, in a cast strung from wires. Months later, the memories would drift back to him in segments. Ellie Troyer and Ricky Niell, encouraging. Bruce Robertson, promising. Abigail Raber, thanking. Cal Troyer, praying. Caroline, smiling bravely.

He would remember hearing the doctors tell Caroline that the leg had been fractured in seven places. They had inserted pins, plates, and screws. One bone fragment had pierced the skin and severed an artery. He had lost a startling amount of blood. Now they could only wait.

In time, they tapered the morphine down. The Percocet left him with an awareness of pain, but without the will to care. He would never remember the wrenching nausea and the unconscious moaning, when the general anesthetic had worn off after the surgery. He would not remember the rotation of cold cloths on his forehead, the alarming drop in the oximeter readings, and the subsequent transfusions. The professor would not likely remember any of these things, or so at least they had told Caroline.

After three days, once it appeared that he was mending, the doctors convinced Caroline to start sleeping at home again. Cal drove her down off the little knoll where Joel Pomerene Hospital sits beside the Wooster road. He turned at the square, and Caroline's eyes filled with tears as they passed the courthouse steps where Nabal Greyson had snapped at the report of a rifle shot, and then pushed the muzzle of his .45 automatic into Branden's face with murderous intent. As Cal's truck climbed the hill to the college, she remembered how Ricky Niell had explained to her that they had had to pry Greyson loose before they could get to Branden to stop the bleeding. She remembered the obliterating avalanche of fear that had buried her when Niell had come in his cruiser to take her to the emergency room. And as Cal turned into the circle where her brick colonial stood on the eastern cliffs of town, she fought to free her mind of the image of Bruce Robertson's sorrowful eyes, when he had met her in his uniform in the hall outside the operating room.

But Professor Branden would likely remember very little of the first days in Joel Pomerene Hospital. He knew that Caroline was there. He knew that the doctors were satisfied. He knew Bruce Robertson was trying to tell him something important about Nabal Greyson.

The fifth day was better. On a warm and breezy afternoon, he awoke to voices. Robertson, Niell, and Cal Troyer were in the room. Branden held his eyes closed and listened to talk of David Hawkins. He heard Cal scoff at something Robertson said, and then he heard Robertson laugh.

Branden pushed up from his pillow, said, "Hawkins didn't miss," and fell back.

There was a warm sponge bath. In another moment, Caroline sat beside him, holding his hand. Blood tests, medication on relentless schedules, and vital signs came in wakeful intervals. Soon he could distinguish night from day, and then the night-shift nurses from the day-shift nurses.

Sometime during it all, when he lay half awake one night, dozing lightly while the night nurses wrote quietly at their desks down the hall, a tall Amish man with blond hair came into his room unobserved. The Amish man carefully removed his wide-brimmed hat, took off a pair of delicate spectacles, laid them on a side table, drew up a chair beside the professor's pillow, and sat down to whisper into Branden's ear. He spoke a greeting in a German dialect, and Branden, with his eyes closed, said, "Herr David Hawkins?"

"Ya, Herr Professor. Aber, Herr David Raber. I am David Raber. I have taken my wife's name."

"Herr Raber." Branden lifted his hand, opened his eyes and turned to see a man with blond hair, cut round, in Dutch style. His face was weathered, and his eyes were clear and peaceful.

"I feared that you wouldn't figure it out in time, Professor."

"You hung the emblem on the microphone stand."

"Yes."

"You never intended to kill Greyson."

"I needed you to believe that I would."

"The emblem exploded as I ran up the steps."

"I rigged it to do that, when it was shot."

"Poetic that you'd choose the motto 'To Serve and Protect'."

"Yes. Greyson betrayed my daughter to Jesse Sands, and he was ex-FBI. The kind of person one ought to be able to expect better of."

"But you never intended to kill him."

"I needed you to believe I would, once you had figured it out. At the very least, I needed to take that shot at Greyson so

Robertson would finally start thinking about why I would want him dead instead of Sands."

"They think you missed and hit the emblem instead of Greyson."

"Let them. They'll never find the bullet anyway."

"I flushed him out for you."

"I couldn't be sure what he'd do after the emblem exploded. I figured you'd believe at first that he'd been shot. I needed you, Professor, to understand what Greyson had done the night Janet was killed."

"He let your daughter die."

"Yes."

"Sands told you that night in the jail?"

"He said Greyson was formerly with the FBI, and I should be wondering how he could have found his way to Janet's house before the police, in their own city, managed to get there themselves. So who was my daughter's greatest betrayer, Professor? Sands who shot her, or Greyson who stood by and let it happen?"

"You had everybody pretty worried when you disappeared after Abigail found the gun in your buggy," Branden said.

"That was not my gun. Greyson was trying to frame me for Bromfield's murder," Hawkins said. "And from what I learned of the sheriff, he pretty well succeeded. Made it so I couldn't just wander into the sheriff's office and tell him about Greyson and Sands without getting myself arrested."

"You could have turned yourself in and let the sheriff sort it all out."

"Professor, if there's one thing I've learned in the service, it's that you never leave your own fate in the hands of others, especially strangers. I figure I had to do things my way."

"You could have killed Greyson on those courthouse steps."

"Mehr doffa net so du, Herr Professor. Murder is forbidden. It is God's privilege to avenge. No one else's."

"You must have been tempted."

"Sorely tempted, Professor," Hawkins said. "At first it was all I could think of."

"You have transcended it all," Branden said.

"By the grace of God, yes. And because of the love of a faithful woman."

"I still don't see that you had to go on the run when Abigail found that pistol."

"Like I said, Professor, that was Greyson's pistol. I had to assume that he was capable of coming after me. Or Abigail, to get to me. So I started shadowing him while he followed you."

"He followed me?" Branden asked.

"You, Cal, and Caroline. Practically everywhere you went. Ricky Niell when he could, too. If I had given him the chance, I believe he would have followed me too, and killed me if necessary. After all, if I was in hiding, who would be surprised if I never showed up again? So I never gave him a chance to find me. Instead, I stalked him until I could figure a way to flush him out. That was also the only way I could make sure that he didn't hurt anyone else."

"And he would have tried to stop us if we had figured out his treachery?"

"I have no doubt."

"Was he ever really that close?"

"One day. You and Niell were in my basement, and he was in the house with you. Upstairs, in a closet. I figure that was about as close as it got."

"You were there, too?"

"In the house, Professor. A sniper's training comes in handy from time to time."

Branden's eyelids fluttered and fell. When he awoke, the blond Amish Raber was still there.

"Can you still hear me, Professor?"

A nod, "Yes."

"I want to tell you about Cal Troyer."

Another nod.

"I saw him two times in Vietnam." Raber faltered, choked back tears and continued. "It's important to me that you know this."

Branden turned, opened his eyes and saw a Dutch face with inestimable peace and strength. Raber's blue eyes held soft pools of tears.

"I was set up, with my spotter, at the edge of a clearing. The chopper had dropped us in two days earlier. The sun was coming up from behind, to our right. On the other side of the clearing, about a hundred and fifty yards away, a footpath emerged from the underbrush, and we were set up there to watch. The target was an NVA colonel. He was to be on that path, at dawn, with his unit. I don't know how we knew he'd be there. We just did. Our orders were to take him at any cost.

"While we lay there in cover, my spotter caught movement at the edge of the clearing about fifty yards up from the path, across from us, to the right. I swung the rifle scope over and there was Cal Troyer, ten feet back from the edge, kneeling. He pulled a soldier's head up, took off his helmet, and gave the man water. Cal was medical. But he stayed there, kneeling. I think they had been there all night, separated from their unit. I watched him through my scope. He knelt in the jungle and prayed."

Raber fought his emotions, but tears came softly as he remembered. "The spotter wanted to call off the shot. We argued. The colonel came into view, and I forced the spotter to range me. He protested, but I took the shot anyway. The last thing I saw as we backed up into the jungle was Cal picking up that wounded soldier, and the dead colonel's men spreading out to search the clearing."

"You betrayed Cal's position?"

"Yes."

"You knew they'd search for you, and likely find only Cal."

"Yes. If I had held off the shot, the unit would have gone on through, and never seen either of us."

"Does Cal know?"

Raber nodded yes, and wept with his eyes buried in his hands. In time, he was able to continue. "We were forced to stay put too long, and missed our primary extraction. Two days later, we hit the secondary, and as we scrambled aboard, the chopper started taking fire from Charlie. As we lifted off, a round nicked something in the hydraulics or the engine, and we started trailing dark smoke. The pilot hollered something back at us, and ten minutes later we set down at an artillery firebase near Chu Lai. Nowhere near our base down south. The battery was shelling the HCM Trail over in Laos, and when our chopper came in low over the mountain in their line of fire, the First Sergeant had to call a ceasefire. We were about two clicks out and coming in smoking hot.

"It was Bravo Battery, 3BN, 18 ARTY. Their 175s were so hot I can remembering seeing one gunner light a smoke off the barrel. They'd been ramming the shells into the breach with steel poles because the hydraulic loaders were two slow to suit them, and there we came, right down their line of fire.

"The pilots took hell from the First Sarge. The motion sensors on the HCM Trail had been lighting up like fireworks all morning, and they'd been throwing everything they had out of the 175s for two hours by the time we shut them down. Penetrators that'd explode deep underground. And the kind that'd detonate overhead, as well. Bouncing Betties. You name it, they threw it at Charlie. Their motto out on the gate read "Bravo Does Make Charlie Hurt." It didn't slow them down any that Firebase Marianne had been completely overrun the day before, and Bravo Battery had it in mind to vaporize everything that moved in Laos that day. By the time we had piled out of the chopper, they had started up again.

"Then, three days later, Cal Troyer staggered in with that

G.I. on his shoulders. I stood in front of a tent and watched him stumble toward the gate. Other guys ran out to help him. They put the G.I. on a stretcher, and Cal walked in on his own.

"I had forgotten about Troyer. Figured him captured and dead. And then he came up to Bravo with that wounded grunt draped over his shoulders."

Raber drew in a labored, clearing breath, leaned back in his chair with his eyes locked on the ceiling, and continued, "Professor, if I had all the words to speak and all the time to speak them, I'd never be able to describe the overwhelming power and majesty that Cal Troyer carried with him that day when he brought that guy into camp."

He stopped, dried his eyes with a handkerchief, and shrugged an apology. He told the rest of it with lines of tears streaming down his cheeks and into his blond chin whiskers, his head shaking slowly side to side.

"I don't know how he made it back, and he's never told me. It could only have been by the grace of God. But I do know this about Cal Troyer. I've known it since the day he carried that kid out of the jungle. It's the reason I came here to Millersburg. You said it yourself, Professor. Cal never gave up on me. Cal Troyer never quits. He doesn't lose hope, and he doesn't give up. Not even on the likes of me.

"When I came here to Millersburg, after leaving the forces, he helped me, even though he knew what I had done in the war. When I finally had the courage to tell him about the colonel in the clearing, he told me he had known for years. He had known, Professor. He took me in, and yet he had known for years that I had betrayed him in Vietnam."

33

Wednesday, July 2

THE white concrete silo had gone up first, four stories high, and then its red metal dome. The masons had traveled from Pennsylvania, but would not stay for the raising. The block foundation had come next, cut into the side of a hill near David and Abigail Raber's little cabin. On the low side, the exposed foundation rose to a height of fifteen blocks. On the high bank, only the top three foundation blocks were exposed above the ground. From there, the slope of the land would give direct access to the second floor of the bank barn.

The lumber had been delivered a week ahead of time. David, Abigail, and her brothers had sorted the boards in the evenings, after they had come in off their fields. They had stacked the boards around the foundation, according to where each type would be needed, and had measured and hammered the wall frames into place on the ground. Most of the wheat had been shocked. The strawberries were in. The corn was as high as a man's chest, and all the gardens in the District were coming along fine.

When the day came, the families of the District began to arrive early, some before daybreak. The men came with their tools, the women with food aplenty. The children came, too, all ages, some with careful instructions, some with special duties, the youngest with gentle admonitions to stand well clear of the work. There would be a noon meal, and the three-story barn, with one long run and a smaller wing attached at the middle, would be finished by 3:00 P.M.

The buggies came onto the Raber farms at the second lane, behind the big house where Abigail's oldest brother lived. Some stopped at the big house, some at the little Daadihaus in the back. Most went straight on over the hill, buggies and wagons alike, past the windmill and down the back pastures. From there, the lane dropped through a field of tall corn, green and luxuriant in a gentle breeze, along a wooden fence line, and into the bottoms. The little lane turned right and followed the edge of a wooded stand of scattered sycamores, along a small stream, and came out at the far end of the glade where Abigail's cabin stood waiting. The families parked their rigs along the fence line, twenty-seven in all before the day was well along, with half a dozen lads assigned to tend the horses at the tether line. The wagons rolled up to the barn, dropped off supplies, and then turned back to unhitch at the fence with the buggies. As the barn went up on the hill, respectable front and back screened porches were added to Abigail's cabin. A cousin brought a white, three-level martin house, with green roofing, and stood it up on a tall iron pole beside the cabin. Women quietly carried in gifts, trying not to be observed doing it. They brought practical household items for the kitchen, linens, sheets, and pillows for the bedroom, and toys for the children to come.

The men were organized loosely by tasks, and by age. Those who didn't swing a hammer or pull a saw carried and stacked wood for those who did. The massive six-by-six walnut uprights went up first along with their bracing frames. The exterior wall frames were poled into place and hammered down. The inside rafters and crossbeams were next. The floorboards were laid as soon as possible on the first level, and then the outer walls and roof were framed out.

As the interlacing wood frame began to rise and take shape, the noises of construction filled the little glade. There were clattering hammers and handsaws that coursed their rhythms through lumber. There were discussions and quiet consultations. The men took to the various tasks, small and large, as if they had all been given their special duty. There was quiet instruction for boys too young to have learned the art of raising a barn.

A small gang of children skittered by, too close to the work, and were scolded away. A half dozen odd tables were set up with drinks and food. An occasional buggy or wagon went back to town for supplies.

On a grassy hill near the cabin, a dozen or so children sat down to play and to watch. The boys all wore straw hats, and the girls bonnets of black or white. All were barefoot, boys and girls alike, as they had been since the day school had let out. The girls' aprons were white in front. The boys' suspenders were uniformly black, straps crossed in back.

Out on a nearby county road, where several cars were parked as locals watched, Mike Branden leaned back against the hood of a new van, crutches propped up under his arms. His jeans on the right leg were split up to the hip, along both the outside and the inside seams, to make room for his cast. His hair was tucked under a broad, straw hat. Caroline was with him, in a long summer dress that closed at the neck, her hair tied in a bun at the back of her head.

They watched as the frame of the barn rose off the foundation in three sections. There would be two long peaks off a roof line that formed a 'T.' As the roofing frame went on, they saw Cal Troyer high up with the older men, nailing down bracing. Next to him, there was a tall, blond Amish man.

As they watched, a black-and-white sheriff's cruiser rolled gently to a stop on the gravel behind their van, and Ricky Niell emerged in uniform, along with Bruce Robertson in civilian casuals. They strolled to the van and joined the Brandens to watch the throng of Amish carpenters below. Robertson took out a pair of binoculars, and Niell gave Branden a knowing smile.

After several minutes scanning the wooden rafters, Robertson said, "Found Cal. Now, where's Hawkins?"

Branden guffawed and said, sarcastically, "Sure Bruce, why don't I just point him out to you? No thanks. Greyson had him framed for murder, and you turned half the county upside down looking for him."

"You two stop it," Caroline scolded.

Robertson winked at her and said, "Can't blame me for trying. I'm not really after him now, anyways. As far as I know, there was no bullet. Just a truck's backfire on the square. Even if there was a shot, I wouldn't arrest Hawkins for it. Got no evidence. Which is probably just how he planned it."

Branden smiled appreciatively at Robertson's restraint.

At the barn raising, nearly half the men could be seen now, coming down out of the rafters to lunch. Half stayed to work. The wallboards were handed up to men hanging in the high frame, and soon the interior walls were being hammered into place. Cal Troyer and David Hawkins were the last to come down off the roof, and Caroline caught the professor's eye to see if he had noticed.

Robertson said, "You know Cal's got the Hawkins house sold."

"For Hawkins?" Branden asked.

Robertson nodded. "You also know that Cal hauled a load of guns up to a gun shop in Wooster and sold them outright for cash?"

"Figures," Branden said.

The exterior walls had started going on, in vertical strips. The interior framing was entirely done. The men trickled back from lunch and some began to lift the heavy oak two-by-eights to others high up in the rafters. The long boards were then shuttled out to the exterior framers, who nailed them into place one at a time, three or four men forming a vertical line to perform the task. Each would hammer in his place, and step back in unison with the others to work on the next board coming up. Then another board would be lifted into place for them, shimmed with a few raps of a hammer, and nailed down. In this fashion, an entire wall was hammered into place, fully two hundred feet by fifteen on the lower story, in less than forty minutes.

As they watched from the hill beside the road, Robertson said, "Marty Holcombe's photographer got pictures that show the city's emblem and our logo hanging on the microphone stand. Now all we can find is dust and splinters."

"No shot, no foul, right, Bruce?" Branden said.

Robertson grinned.

Branden changed the subject. "I understand you're holding Greyson."

Robertson nodded and said, "Let's start with his little fracas with you. There's two counts of carrying a concealed weapon, one of aggravated assault, and attempted murder, and that's just the day he hammered you. The aggravated felony assault will stick. Don't know about attempted murder. Doesn't matter, though. I'm pretty sure he also killed Bromfield. The coroner has matched the powder burns on Bromfield's temple with the live rounds we found in the gun you brought in."

"How do you know it was Greyson's pistol?" Branden asked. "There weren't any fingerprints."

"No prints that were obvious," Robertson said. "But you know those Rugers? The way the hammer springs are wedged into the pistol's grip at the backstrap? Difficult to reinsert? Well, we had a gunsmith disassemble the thing and lifted a print of Greyson's index finger off the spring housing."

Branden whistled in admiration. "Have you got the warden at Trenton figured out yet?"

"Yeah, Mike. I've got that SOB. Turns out that when I first called him after Bromfield's murder, asking about Jesse Sands, he withheld mention of Nabal Greyson's name. He knew they were connected, big time—Greyson and Sands, and he should have come across with that. But he should also have suspected about Eric Bromfield. Just kept his mouth shut and made us put it all together ourselves. He's going to lose his job by the time we get done with him in the newspapers."

"I got the stonewall from him, too. His lieutenant figured different, and sent me that fax," Branden said.

"And Jesse Sands?" Caroline asked.

"He's already down at Lucasville," Robertson said.

Niell stirred and said, "I've got to start a shift." He glanced a question to Robertson.

Robertson asked Branden, "Can I catch a ride in that new prairie wagon you've got there?"

Caroline said, "Sure, Bruce." Robertson waved Niell on, and Niell drove away toward Millersburg.

Now, the roofing boards were going down on the peaks. Robertson lifted his binoculars to his eyes, scanned and said, "Tall fellow working next to Cal."

Branden said, "So?"

"Tall, blond Amish men are about as common as thirsty fish."

Branden shot Robertson a look.

"Just want to meet the fellow, Mike. Cal wasn't any help at all, but Hawkins did me a favor. Put me onto Greyson for Bromfield."

"That's all Hawkins ever wanted to do, Bruce." Branden gazed a while longer, then turned to Caroline, and signaled her by tilting his head in the direction of the cabin in the glade. She made an excuse about the women at the cabin and walked down the slope.

Branden turned to Robertson and said, "Bruce, you were wrong about Hawkins at first, and you were wrong to doubt Cal at all."

Robertson gave a snide protest. "Cal could have helped more."

"Hawkins and Cal are cut from the same cloth, Bruce."

"So?"

"Do you have any idea what Cal did in Vietnam?"

"Medic. So what?"

"Do you know that he holds medals from that war?"

"Yes."

"The Congressional Medal of Honor?"

Robertson covered his surprise, but not before the professor saw the truth in his eyes. "Sure," Robertson said, offhand.

"You didn't know," Branden asserted. "Cal's never told anyone about it. I didn't know until Hawkins told me.

"Bruce, you're having trouble seeing Cal for who he is, because you grew up with him. All you can see is a kid, an old playground friend."

Robertson began to argue, but the professor cut him off with an upraised palm.

"No, Bruce. It's true. When you were first hunting Hawkins, you were harder on Cal than he deserved." He waited a moment while he looked sternly into the sheriff's eyes, and then he continued. "You played a cowboy song for me about a horse the other day."

"Ian Tyson. 'Milk River Ridge,'" Robertson said, glad for the change of subject.

"And why'd you say you liked it?" Branden asked gently.

"Competence. Courage. Fidelity. Steadfastness."

"Right, Bruce. The kind of trustworthiness a man can depend on."

"And?"

"And that's what Cal Troyer has been doing these last few years for David Hawkins." He let the sheriff mull that over and watched the barn finish up.

Most of the men were down from the roof. There was still a scattering of work inside, but overhead the roof was finished. As the men gathered their tools and looked their work over, two remained on the peak, Cal Troyer standing next to a tall, blond Amish man with a deep farmer's tan.

Robertson stood quietly beside the professor and turned his thoughts inward. He watched Cal shake the tall man's hand on the rooftop, and he watched them climb down together from the peak.

Branden took up his point again. "At first, you thought Hawkins had killed Eric Bromfield and was planning to kill Jesse Sands. But did you ever bother to find out what Sands said to Hawkins that night at the jail? What it was that set Hawkins off?"

"I suppose you're gonna tell me, now."

"I can tell you word for word," Branden said with confidence, "but I'd rather tell you what Sands meant. Essentially, Sands told Hawkins to think it through and he'd see that someone else was responsible for her murder. He said that his killing her wasn't the worst betrayal, even though he had pulled the trigger."

"We know Sands killed her." Robertson said, interested.

"How do we know that?"

"Greyson caught him running out of the house."

"Right. Now, when Lieutenant Brown of the Trenton State Prison sent me that fax, I found out that Greyson was tracking Sands because Sands had raped and institutionalized his fiancée."

"That's not new, Mike."

"He was there, Bruce, when Sands went into that house. And when Janet Hawkins went in later."

Robertson nodded. "He beat our guys to Sands."

"Seems a bit unlikely, doesn't it, Bruce? A stranger arrives on a 911 before the police can get there, in their own town? He must have been there all along. From the first."

Robertson cursed.

Branden continued. "He followed Sands there and then stood outside as Sands shot Janet Hawkins. That let him capture Sands for a murder, when he otherwise would have had him only for breaking and entering."

Robertson cursed vehemently.

"So," Branden said, "Greyson's betrayal of Janet Hawkins was more appalling than her murder. Greyson murdered Eric Bromfield because Eric had put Sands and Greyson together, and if that became known, it wouldn't have been long before you would have asked what Greyson had been doing there that night, before the police arrived."

"I once told Sands I'd be glad to throw a switch on him," Robertson said. "Seems now like we ought to do Greyson first. As it stands, though, the state's going to save some money on Greyson."

Branden waited for an explanation.

Robertson said, "Have you ever talked to Greyson?"

"Twice," Branden said. "The second time under less than pleasant circumstances."

"Notice his voice? Scratchy?"

"Yes."

"He's got throat cancer," Robertson said. "By the time he's been sentenced on the weapons charges, not to mention the Bromfield murder, the man will be bedridden. Nabal Greyson is going to die, in jail, of throat cancer, before the end of the year."

Branden shook his head distastefully.

Caroline came up the grassy slope toward them, her long dress caught by a gentle afternoon breeze. The work on the barn was finished. Buggies were loaded up and driven slowly away, back along the lane, past the stand of sycamores, and up over the rise near the windmill. Soon, there remained only the immediate family of Rabers, forty-seven in all, and the men began to gather in front of the cabin and on the cabin's new front porch.

Caroline reached them and said, "I spoke to Abigail Raber. We're invited to supper."

Robertson asked, "Can I get a lift into town, first?"

Caroline said, "You too, Bruce."

"You're kidding."

"Abigail and David Raber have invited you, themselves," Caroline said. "You're invited, Bruce, along with us."

Near the cabin, Cal Troyer stood up and encouraged them down the slope with a wave of his arm.

As they walked down the slope, Robertson asked, "You still going to fire your cannon, Mike? Fourth of July?"

Caroline said, forcefully, "Oh, no, he's not."

Branden shrugged and tapped at his cast. "Can't haul the thing out to the cliffs."

As they walked in tall grass toward the Raber cabin, Robertson said, "Cal and I will haul it out for you, Mike. Seems I need to have a long talk with the pastor, after all."

Q & A with Author P. L. Gaus

Q: Holmes County is known as the home of one of the world's largest Amish communities. What is the history of how the Amish arrived in Ohio?

A: The first Amish people settled in Ohio in 1807. This was a group led by Jakob Miller, who was sent by earlier colonists from Somerset County, Pennsylvania. Miller and company made the journey by river routes, all the way to Iowa, searching for a new homeland, before turning back along a land route that took them through the Killbuck Valley in Holmes County. They thought this was a perfect location for their new homes, and they staked their claim to land there. It has grown over the centuries to become the largest Anabaptist settlement in the world. The nearly fifty separate Amish and Mennonite sects that live in this area now, mostly in the hills and valleys southeast of Apple Creek and east and south of Millersburg, have emigrated from dozens of locations in Germany, Switzerland, and the Alsace region. For instance, Samuel Mueller brought 192 followers to Philadelphia in November 1763, all from the canton of Bern, Switzerland. As another example, there is the group led by Michael Neuenschwander, who traveled from Alsace, through Paris, New York, and Pittsburgh, to settle in Ohio in 1823. The journey took six months, and it is typical of the routes followed by many hundreds of other congregations, all looking for religious freedom in America.

Q: How did you write the Amish and English characters for your novels?

A: I have written the Amish characters in my novels to illustrate the scripture passage or religious tenet on which each story is based. As a result, the Amish characters are different in each novel, and I have placed them into my settings and plots so that I can illuminate that scripture passage or principle that serves as the focus for a deep moral dilemma. In *Broken English,* Abigail Raber is betrothed to an English man who is challenged by one of the most dreadful temptations for revenge that a person could face. Will he remain true to the faith he has chosen, or will he revert to the soldier he once was, in order to avenge his daughter?

For the English regulars in my novels, I wrote three men to serve as the *sleuths.* I tried to pen these as a single character when I first started writing, but I soon realized that no single person could accomplish all that I wanted from my protagonists. So, first I have Professor Michael Branden, and his wife Caroline, who often has insights that surpass her husband's. Then there is Sheriff Bruce Robertson, along with all of the law enforcement actors who would need to take part in a criminal investigation. Third there is Pastor Caleb "Cal" Troyer, who serves as a handy intermediary between English and Amish societies, which are so complexly intertwined throughout all of Holmes County. Cal is essential to my stories, because Amish ways and beliefs are often completely inscrutable to English people. Bruce serves as my gruff and heavy-handed lawman. Michael, the professor, is the thinker who often finds himself at the center of an investigation, where an understanding of Amish culture is essential to unraveling the mystery. The stories are also populated with the people who are important in the lives of my three protagonists, and the whole package helps my readers understand what it is like to live Amish, to think Amish, and to pray Amish.

It is my goal to bring my readers closely and intimately into Amish society, and to help them understand what Amish life is all about.

Broken English:

Q: *Broken English* begins with an epigraph citing scripture from Romans 12:17–19. What is the significance of these lines, both in the context of Amish culture generally and in David Hawkins's story in particular?

A: This scripture is a severe injunction against vengeance. It is one of the most important passages in the Bible for understanding the absolute conviction of all Amish people that pacifism is the only Godly course in life. For David Hawkins, who has just recently found his way into a life of pacifism, there is then the awful temptation to do what he had always done best, in his former life in combat—to take revenge, killing Jesse Sands. The moral quandary of the novel is therefore David's. Will he fall from grace so soon after converting to the Amish faith, or will he hold fast against the nearly unopposable impulse to seek revenge?

One parallel to this verse of scripture is found in Hebrews 10:31, which reads:

For we know Him who said:
"It is mine to avenge; I will repay,"
And again:
"The Lord will judge His people."
It is a dreadful thing to fall into the hands of
the living God.

In other words, God stands opposed to human vengeance, and Amish people take this to be an absolute command. In fact, God has declared here that he reserves vengeance to himself, stating explicitly that His vengeance is a dreadful thing. So, I wrote *Broken English* to show that David Hawkins held true to this scriptural command, whereas Jesse Sands and Nabal Greyson did not, and the consequences for David are quite different from those for Sands and Greyson.

Q: This volume of your Amish mystery series features an English character who has converted to Amish faith. How common are such conversions in Amish culture? Are the Amish typically welcoming of outsiders who embrace their religion and lifestyle?

A: Amish people in general are not particularly evangelistic. Mennonite people are different, and they support missionaries all over the world. But Amish people do not go looking for converts. Nevertheless, there are rare examples of English persons who have admired Amish culture and lifestyle to the point where they have sought to join a congregation. When this happens, the Amish bishops are generally welcoming and helpful. But everyone involved knows that this is a questionable undertaking. Amish life is extraordinarily difficult for people raised English, and cultural rules for congregants are so severe that few English people have made the conversion successfully. I know one fellow who was raised among the Amish and who knew quite well what it would take to live an Amish life. He found himself in love with an Amish girl, and he converted some fifty years ago in order to marry her. When I first met him, he had held true to Amish faith throughout all the years of his long marriage. But cases like this are rare, and English people who have tried to live as Amish have failed more often than not.

Discussion Questions for Reading Groups

1. In what ways are the English characters in this story, including Jesse Sands, David Hawkins, and Nabal Greyson, examples of "Broken English"? What are some possible interpretations of this phrase?

2. Why might some English people hold animosity for the Amish, and what are some instances of this animosity in the story?

3. How is the character Abigail Raber, an Amish woman, portrayed in *Broken English*? What might be some of the reasons for Abigail's many sorrows?

Excerpt from

Clouds without Rain

Book 3 in the Amish Country Mysteries

1

Monday, August 7
4:15 P.M.

PROFESSOR Michael Branden, driving a black Amish buggy, worked his horse at a walk along Walnut Creek Township Lane T-414, just north of Indian Trail Creek in Holmes County, Ohio, on a sweltering Monday afternoon early in August. Coming up to one of the short stretches of blacktop laid in front of a house to cut the dust, he slowed the horse and rolled gently onto the pavement. The buggy rocked and swayed from side to side on its light oval springs, and the iron wheels cut sharp lines through the tar blisters in the blacktop. The horse's hooves gave hollow plopping sounds that switched back to a lighter clicking in the dust and gravel after the blacktop played out beyond the house. The sky was cloudless, the sun hot, and beyond the thin line of trees that bordered the lane, the fields seemed withered and spent, the crops stricken with thirst.

Branden was dressed to outward appearance as an Amishman. The Amish clothes and broad-brimmed straw hat with a flat crown were his own, bought two summers before, when he had worked on a kidnapping case involving an Amish child. He was wearing shiny blue denim trousers over leather work boots, a dark blue shirt with the sleeves rolled up to his elbows, and a black cloth vest, unfastened in front.

Under his vest, he had hooked a deputy sheriff's wallet badge over the belt he wore instead of the traditional suspenders, a concession to English style so that the heavy badge and three

1

pairs of handcuffs would ride securely at his waist. The belt also held a beeper, though locating a phone in those parts of the county would be a task.

The professor brought the rig to a stop, took off his straw hat, poured a little water from a plastic bottle over his wavy brown hair, and rubbed at it vigorously. Then he laid his hat on the seat, and while he dried his tanned face and neck with a red bandanna, he straightened the rest of the gear riding beside him.

There was a black radio handset from the sheriff's department, turned off for the task at hand. A Holmes County map from the county engineer's office, folded to the square of Walnut Creek Township. An elaborate Contax RTS III SLR camera with a long Zeiss lens, tucked securely into the corner of the buggy seat. On the floorboards under the seat, a Smith and Wesson Model 60 .357 Magnum revolver in a black leather holster.

With a light slap of the reins, Branden started the horse again. About a hundred yards further up the lane, he pulled into the drive of a new two-story Amish house and stepped the horse to a stone watering trough. A door on the upper floor opened as he stopped. Lydia Shetler, dressed in a plain, dark-blue dress and black bonnet, came out onto the top porch of the house and asked, "Any luck, already?" with the classic Dutch accent of the region.

The professor shook his head and said, "Mind if I water the horse?"

Lydia intoned, "If it suits you," and leaned over with her elbows on the porch rail to watch.

The porch, set on tall posts, was level with the second floor of the house. The area under this high porch was latticed in front with a rose arbor, which made a shady breezeway at ground level. The family's laundry was hung out for the day, drying on clotheslines in the breezeway.

Branden climbed out, and as the horse snorted and drank water, Lydia asked, "How much longer do you figure to make these rides, yet, Herr Professor?"

"Till we get them," Branden said and laughed. He slapped his hat at the dust on his ankles and added, "Or until the sheriff gets bored with the idea."

Lydia nodded as if to say that she understood the sheriff's impulsiveness well enough, and asked, "Are you sure only our two families know about your business?"

"Why? Have you heard anything on the gossip mill?"

"Not a word."

"Then I suppose I'll still keep riding. As long as nobody at either end lets it slip."

"I haven't heard any mention," Lydia repeated, and went back inside. Branden mounted into the buggy, swung around on the wide gravel lane, and walked her out to T-414 again, continuing east toward the little burg of Trail.

This was his fifth afternoon drive in two weeks, traveling the northern edges of Walnut Creek Township on the center-east edge of Holmes County. His assignment was to be the decoy in Sheriff Bruce Robertson's strategy to catch the two Amish-clad teenagers who were making a reputation for themselves that summer by robbing the Peaceful Ones. Disguised in rubber goat's-head masks, they rode up to the slow-moving buggies on their mountain bikes and demanded money. Surprisingly large sums had been involved, and Sheriff Robertson now had his decoy in place. Professor Michael Branden, Civil War History, Millersburg College, a duly sworn reserve deputy, with a buggy, a costume of Amish clothes, a radio, an ample supply of handcuffs, and a very expensive camera. Also a revolver, just in case.

As the professor rattled along slowly in his buggy, a pickup shot by in the opposing lane. In the cloud of dust left in its wake, two Amish teenagers passed from behind on mountain bikes. Branden took up his camera and fired off several frames on motor drive.

Branden tensed a bit, wondering what he would actually do if the young bandits ever did approach him demanding money. He wasn't at all certain that the sheriff was right about this

3

one. Amish or English, they wouldn't be that easy to apprehend. "They're Amish, Mike," Robertson had said. "They'll just stand there when you show them your badge." And if he took their picture or stepped down from the buggy to confront them? What then? They'd take off on their bikes.

That'd be it, Branden thought dourly. They'd scatter, and he wouldn't have a chance of chasing them down in the heat. The professor shook his head, laughed halfheartedly, and wondered about the ribbing he'd take from the regular deputies if the sheriff's little game should play out as he suspected it might, with him giving chase through fields or over hills, losing them both.

Chagrined, Branden rode the rest of his shift haphazardly back and forth along T-414, radio off so as not to give him away. As the supper hour approached, he headed south on T-412 to return the buggy to its owner. As he brought the buggy into the Hershbergers' drive, one of the middle sons, Ben, stepped out of a woodshop at the side of the property, slapping sawdust off his long denim apron. He waved to Branden and came down the steps to a hitching rail beside the gravel drive. The drive curved gently around a well-tended volleyball court and dropped with the slope of the land into a wide valley, passing the north side of a weathered white house. Three stories and gabled, the historic building had a round sitting room and cone-shaped roof set at the corner, where a large covered porch began at the front and wrapped around the side. Grandmother Hershberger sat peacefully in an oak rocker on the elevated porch, a small mound of potatoes on the floor at her side, peeling long, curling skins into her lap. Branden tipped his hat, and she glanced briefly at him with reserved acknowledgment. As Ben came forward and took the horse by the bridle, Branden turned on his handset radio and heard Sheriff Bruce Robertson shouting, "Two ambulances. Maybe three! Hell, Ellie, send five."

"Fire's on their way, Sheriff," Ellie Troyer said, her voice frayed with tension.

"It's a mess, Ellie," Robertson's voice cracked staccato over the radio. "One buggy, maybe more. Can't tell yet. A semi jack-knifed. Cab upside down in the ditch. The trailer has taken out at least one car and it's burning now," followed by, "For crying out loud, Ellie, where are my squads?"

"On their way," Ellie said, managing to sound calm.

"Schrauzer's unit is up there right in the middle of the whole thing," Robertson shouted into the microphone. "Can't see him anywhere. Going closer, Ellie. Get those fire trucks down here NOW!"

The mic clicked off for a minute or so and then Robertson called in again, more subdued. "Get the coroner, too, Ellie."

Branden pulled his buggy up sharply, set the hand brake, scrambled down onto the driveway, and took the radio off the buggy seat. He paced in a circle on the drive as he made his call. "This is Mike Branden. Over."

Ellie's voice came back. "Signal 39."

"Township 412 at the Hershbergers." As he spoke, he gathered his things from the buggy and walked quickly to his small pickup.

"It's right there, Professor," Ellie said. "You're practically on top of it. 515 south of Trail."

"Roger that," Branden said and started his engine. "515 south of Trail. Ellie, I'll be right there!"

He pulled the door closed, fish-tailed on the gravel lane, waved at Ben, and heard Robertson come over the radio.

"Mike, you come in from the north. South of Trail. That'll put you on the other side. I'm farther south, the other side of the pileup, and I need someone on your side to stop traffic."

"I'm coming up on Trail now," Branden said, steering with his left hand, holding the handset to his ear with the right.

"Turn right at Trail, Mike," Robertson said. "Slow. We're down in a little valley and if you don't come in slow, you'll run us all over."

Branden dropped south out of Trail on 515, came around a sharp curve and over a hill, and saw a tall plume of black smoke beyond the next rise in the road. He came up to the top of the hill, stopped abruptly, stepped out of the truck, and leaned forward on the open door, shaken by what he saw some hundred yards below.

A semitrailer rig sprawled across the road, the cab overturned in the right-hand ditch, the trailer laid across the road on its side, its rear wheels spinning slowly over the left-hand ditch. The truck driver lay twisted on the pavement beside the overturned cab.

A monstrous gasoline fire engulfed a sedan pinned under the far side of the trailer, and dense smoke drifted up and trailed west over a field of stunted corn. The flames leaped from the road to the grasses in the roadside ditches and spread rapidly into the withered crops in the fields on each side of the road. Even at this distance from the wreckage, Branden could smell the smoke and the gasoline. He heard a car approaching behind him and turned to stop it with a palm held outward. A second car pulled up, and then a third. He took up a position to block the passing lane and turned back to view the wreckage.

Just beyond the burning sedan was Phil Schrauzer's cruiser. Something long and bulky had punched through the windshield. Further back there was a line of two pickups and a produce truck, all apparently uninvolved in the wreck. Two of the three drivers stood helplessly beside their trucks. The third had stooped to open a briefcase on the pavement. As Branden watched, the man took a cell phone out of the briefcase, stood sweating profusely while he dialed a number, and talked as he turned his head this way and that, looking with astonishment at the wreckage that lay around him. The man fixed his gaze on the house at the end of the driveway, spoke for a moment longer, switched off the cell phone, and dialed another call. He spoke for perhaps a minute, listened briefly, and tossed the phone into the briefcase on the pavement. Kneeling down, he closed the case, and stood to drop it through the open window onto the front seat of his pickup.

The sheriff's black-and-white 4x4 was stopped in the passing lane beside the produce truck, door hanging ajar. Another sheriff's unit was parked at the top of the next hill, turning cars back toward Walnut Creek. A cruiser from the state highway patrol came past the roadblock and pulled in behind Robertson's 4x4.

Branden stepped over to his pickup, reached in under the seat, pulled out binoculars, and turned the dial back to a full wide-angle view. He turned momentarily to check on the line of cars and trucks that had stacked up behind him and saw that his roadblock was self-regulating, as some cars turned back to find another route.

When he first held the binoculars to his eyes, black smoke filled the eyepiece. He trained right and found the bottom of the overturned cab, its front wheels hanging awkwardly in the air, the driver motionless on the ground. He moved the binoculars up and left and found Robertson waving the state trooper closer to the fire.

Robertson pushed toward the fire with his forearm over his eyes and reached Deputy Schrauzer's cruiser. Branden cringed as he saw the sheriff start to work at whatever had pierced the windshield, struggling to pull it back out with his left hand, while he tried to steady Schrauzer with his right hand through the driver's-side window.

The fire in front of Robertson flared violently, and Branden, startled by the massive orange fireball, sucked in air through his teeth and stumbled backward. There was a shattering crack of glass as flames expanded out and upward. Robertson turned his back and bent low beside the cruiser, shielding himself from the flames. But after a few seconds the big sheriff lumbered up onto the hood of the cruiser, and the trooper dashed up to take charge of Schrauzer, still pinned in his seat. As writhing gasoline flames spread toward Robertson, the sheriff pulled what looked like a tight bundle of wooden poles out of the windshield. He tossed it onto the pavement beside the cruiser and climbed down from the hood. Shirt ablaze, he helped the trooper drag Schrauzer out of the cruiser and along the pavement, away from the flames. Once Schrauzer was clear of further danger, Robertson threw himself onto his back and rolled from side to side, while the trooper beat at the flames with his hat.

There was another flare-up over the burning car, and Branden heard the first squad's sirens out on the Walnut Creek hill. The ambulance crested the hill, sped into the valley, and went directly past the trucks to where Robertson and the trooper crouched beside Schrauzer, who was laid out on his back.

Branden watched as the highway patrolman began to help Robertson out of his uniform shirt, still smoldering. Robertson bent suddenly backward and appeared to cry out in pain as the shirt stuck to the skin on his back. A paramedic hurried forward and cut the shirt loose from patches that had fused to ugly burns on the sheriff's back. Nancy Blain, in jeans and a T-shirt, stood back from the sheriff, snapping photos for the *Holmes Gazette*.

A team of paramedics loaded Schrauzer into an ambulance and headed back toward Millersburg. Robertson turned and surveyed the crash scene, as a paramedic from a second squad tended burns on the sheriff's back and arms.

Branden watched Robertson, bare-chested, directing fire department volunteers to the burning car, with pieces of his uniform shirt clinging to his back. The sheriff took a step toward the fire, and the paramedic pulled him back by the arm. Gratefully, Branden sensed that Robertson seemed content to stand back and let the squads do their jobs.

The first fire truck to arrive had started laying foam on the burning car. Nancy Blain darted here and there among the wreckage, taking photos with her black Nikon. Up on the hill behind the wreck, the professor trained his binoculars on the ground at Robertson's feet, then in wider circles on the ground in front of the semi. In every direction on the opposing hill, both on the pavement where Robertson stood and sprayed over the vehicles and terrain not directly damaged by the impact of the crash, Branden saw a vast scattering of black fabric and wooden splinters. Back up the hill there lay a thin axle. Smashed and twisted buggy wheels lay in the ditch beyond, two of them still attached to a second bent axle. The largest fragment of the buggy lay in the field at the edge of the road, some twenty yards away from the cab of the semi. In its tangled mass, Branden made out the torn and twisted fabric of Amish attire. Nancy Blain's slender figure came into view, as she aimed her camera at the buggy. She lingered for several shots there and then stood and began firing off frame after frame as she pivoted full circle in place.

A second pumper arrived on the scene. Having extinguished the fires at the car, the firefighters ran their heavy hoses out into the burning fields and sprayed a broad arc of water on the out-lying ridges of fire burning through the crops. Branden looked again for Robertson, and found him kneeling beside the road, near the overturned cab of the truck.

He was holding the head of the downed horse by its bridle. The horse's back legs had been mauled by the impact, and the right hind leg was torn loose at the hip. The horse's coat was matted with blood and its flesh was ripped open, exposing the bowels. The front legs of the horse pawed uselessly at the air. Branden saw Robertson draw his sidearm and point it at the head of the horse. There was a puff of smoke at the muzzle, fol-lowed abruptly by the report of the gun, and the horse lay im-mediately still.